MW00936505

Soulmate

Kellie McAllen

ISBN: 1512231908
ISBN-13: 978-1512231908

Chapter One

Prologue

The womb should have been a perfect place for a soul to grow a body. Perhaps most wombs were a sanctuary of warmth and peace, with soft murmurs of love whispering through the walls and the gentle sway of life rocking the soul into gentle slumber. This womb, unfortunately, had not been so idyllic. Angry voices, drunken movements, and the bitter taste of stress flooded the womb and left the little soul on edge, anxious tension his constant companion. It came as no surprise when his departure held the same intensity.

The day begins as any other. He wakes to apprehension; his mother's distaste for him a tangible anguish. Yet a sort of relief comes briefly to his senses as they travel, and a bud of hope begins to blossom that perhaps she has finally made peace with his existence. His mother enters the clinic with resoluteness in her spine and the thrill of freedom in her soul. She doesn't think about the soul within her, what will happen as its half-formed body is torn from her womb. He doesn't know enough about the world to recognize that her release is his destruction. In one sharp moment, the blackness overtakes him and his soul floats free from the flesh to which he once belonged. Suddenly, a rush of light pulls him back into consciousness and he awakens once again in a place just the same yet different from the one before.

Tension contracts his muscles, and his limbs flail uselessly as the body accommodates his intrusion. He sees his hands reach and grasp, the tiny fingers waving, but he can't move them like he used to; they have a life of their own. The soft pink walls surround him as before, but the sensation is altogether different, as if he were merely a spectator in this world and no longer a participant, his mind still strong and active, but his body a useless weight. Slowly, awareness dawns, and he discovers he is not alone. There is someone else sharing his tiny universe.

In her dreams she finally finds him. She is surprised by his arrival, but no longer frightened. She can sense his gentle nature. He is happy to be with her, in his new home, so much more peaceful than his first. He feels the love of her mother and her pleasure at their presence, hears her singing tender lullabies and speaking to them in reverent tones. In slumber, his companion remembers all the tranquil days she has spent, growing and becoming, basking in her mother's love. Eventually he shows her his first memories, but they disturb her, and instead he replays the happy times they've shared together. Months go by, and although they do not understand time yet, they know they are changing rapidly. Each day brings new awareness, new sensations, and they sense an eagerness in their mother, an anticipation of change soon to come.

The day began differently than all the others, with pain wracking their mother's body, the walls of her womb contracting, squeezing, jostling them, their mother's cries sharp and terrifying, accompanying each fearsome spasm. The attacks continued through the day and into the night, growing longer and more violent, till they thought their world would collapse upon them, crushing them with the weight of their mother's agony. But instead, all at once their world expands.

Sound, once the soothing rhythm of life, pulsing gently outside — now invades, harsh and piercing, ripping wide the barrier, flooding them with sensation. The light consumes them, touch awakens their skin, and they cry out. The sound of their own voice frightens and astounds, setting off a torrent of cries, until they are swaddled in blankets and laid to rest, the familiar thrum of their mother's heart once again drowning out the chaos around them. The child settles into slumber on her mother's breast, and her companion plays back the first moments of their life for her, reliving the wonder and the terror. His first chance at life ended before it began, but his second chance had begun in earnest, an exhilarating explosion of sights and sounds and textures. He didn't know yet that he wasn't really living, his chance at life already forfeited, his destiny tied up in hers.

Chapter Two

The toddler slept fitfully, it seemed, ever since the beginning. Her eyes fluttered, limbs twitched, half-formed words bubbled from her little mouth as if she were dreaming from the moment she laid down until the harsh rush of morning pulled her from her slumber. Her parents wondered what she could be dreaming about as she cooed and gurgled, arms and legs flailing as if her dreams held more excitement that the reality of her bucolic life. They didn't know about her companion; how he filled her dreams with play and whimsy, the two friends free to frolic in the playground of her mind. The child knew no different, for it seemed her friend had always been with her, sharing every moment, only to relive it with her every time she slept.

The stowaway soul longed to be "the daddy" in Rachel's playtime fantasy. The girl spent all her free time carrying a tattered baby doll, making pretend dinners for her stuffed animal family, and trying to coax their exasperated feline, Maxie, into playing her part in the drama. Many nights, the soul created his own stories for her night-

Soulmate

time pleasure, and he relished in her delight at his flights of fancy, but the boy loved when the girl continued her play in her dreams. He thought if she could include toys and animals in her fantasy, surely she could include him someday. So far, however, a barrier had separated them. He knew she was aware of him, that he lived in her body and saw the world through her eyes. In her dreams, he showed her what he saw, and she could feel his joy and pain at her experiences like he could feel hers, but the two had not yet learned to communicate with each other, and the little soul yearned for the chance to speak to her and her to him. But he had no voice, no mouth with which to speak, no name by which he could be known.

Maybe that was the answer, he thought: a name for her to call him. Human language was full of nomenclature, they were learning. Everything that mattered had a label. Her parents often pointed out items she came across and told her what they were and what to call them. Like treasures collected in a hope chest, the child collected words in her vocabulary for things that mattered, things she recognized, and things that had a purpose in her world. How could she recognize that he was someone, when there was no name for what he was? A watcher for one thing, a companion, but neither of those words encompassed all he was.

Rachel's fantasy turned to memory as she thought back on her favorite day. It was summer, and her mother had been granted a reprieve from her duties for the day. With her feminine wiles she had persuaded the girl's father to watch his daughter for the afternoon so she could indulge in some much-needed pampering. She had gone to the spa for a manicure and to the mall for a new outfit, and Daddy had been given carte blanche as long as he didn't call her unless it was an absolute emergency. Being the doting father that he was, Daddy had given in quite whole-heartedly to Rachel's cries for ice cream and playtime, and the two were soon buckled in the van and on their way to the neighborhood park, stopping only to acquire double scoops of Blue Moon. The day was brilliant, with sunshine sparking on everything from their fancy new van to the rusty old slide in the middle of the playground. They laughed and sang at the top of their lungs as the breeze through the windows twisted her honey blonde hair into crazy knots and the ice cream dripped on their shirts, making Rorschach blobs that Mommy would have criticized but Daddy didn't seem to notice, let alone mind.

Rachel's favorite thing to do on the playground was swing, and Mommy usually obliged, but she had the caution of any new mother and rarely let Rachel fly as high as she'd like. Daddy, however, was much less cautious, and seemed to consider the swings a challenge to his arm strength and the laws of gravity. Higher and higher, the swing would rise with each thrust, till her bottom came off the seat and the chains began to swing wildly, sending her spinning in all directions, laughing and crying till she felt like the ice cream would leap from her belly and her eyes were teary from the sting of the wind. When Rachel was dizzy and weak-kneed from swinging, the two piled back in the van and headed for home.

Seeing this memory in the girl's mind, with sudden clarity the boy realized his role in her life. She was the driver, controlling their body and navigating their path, and he was the passenger. Like Rachel, delighting in the thrill of her swing ride, he too was a rider in her mind. As a passenger, he had a front seat view of every exciting moment, and perhaps he could even inspire the destination, but she would always hold the keys. He was a rider, and that would be his name. With his new identity firm in his mind, the rider strove to reveal himself to the girl.

He filled her dream with rapid-fire images of her begging Mommy and Daddy to take her for a ride — in the car, on the swings, on the miniature pony they once saw at the fair, on the lawn mower, even on Daddy — piggyback style. Rachel giggled at the happy memories, but she didn't understand the message he was trying to show her. These memories only showed her as the rider, not him. If only he could show her himself, maybe then she would understand. With all his might, he tried to visualize a similar image in her mind, only instead of her begging Daddy for a ride, he put himself in her place: him begging her to push the swing a little higher, spin the merry-go-round a little faster, put another quarter in the bucking horse in front of the grocery store. At first, Rachel was baffled by this role reversal, but as the rider began to light with joy as the Rachel in his dream said yes to one more piggyback ride and one more trip to the ice cream shop, she began to understand.

"You want to go for a ride?" Rachel asked of her invisible companion, the first time she'd ever tried to speak directly to him. Fear and excitement coursed through her as she realized that her companion was trying to communicate with her on a level more direct than ever before.

Emboldened by the thrill of his accomplishment, the rider thought his name over and over again, with every ounce of strength that he had. "Rider, Rider, Rider, Rider...." The name crashed through his thoughts like waves on the beach till their every heartbeat pumped in rhythm to it.

"Rider?" The word burst from her mind and out of her mouth, waking her from her dream and forcing her upright, eyes wide with enchantment. The girl scanned her room excitedly, searching for her companion, but only his name had materialized on her lips. Disappointed her friend had not become a real life playmate but still thrilled he had spoken to her at all, Rachel began to chatter enthusiastically to him.

"Rider?... like, you're going for a ride with me? I like to go for rides! You ride with me all the time, too, dontcha? How did you get in there, Rider? Can you ever come out? Can you come out and play with me? You would be fun to play with!"

The questions tumbled from her faster and faster as her excitement grew, and Rider could hardly keep up with them all, let alone try to answer them. Instead, he resorted to flashback images of her playtime: her playing the mommy and the daddy with Maxie as their insolent child, her substituting her great big teddy bear for the daddy instead, until finally he conjured an image of a little boy, perhaps someone she'd seen on TV or at the playground one day, but no one she really knew. He pictured the two of them playing house in her bedroom, her little table set with plastic plates and cups and the two of them chatting like grownups about the weather and the plans for the day and how baby Maxie was fussy and wouldn't eat her oatmeal. Her stuffed animals occupied the other chairs and he imagined himself spooning cereal into their mouths and wiping their chins while he told Rachel about the important meeting he had that day and she described her plans to take the children to the pool after she did the grocery shopping and made their lunch.

Rachel clapped her hands and squealed with delight at his make-believe scene. He knew just how to play with her! She quickly jumped from her bed and ran to the miniature kitchen in the corner of her room. Setting up the table just how he had imagined it, she began to chatter back and forth with Rider, developing their fantasy. Their play became so animated and Rachel's voice so loud, that eventually her mother got curious and poked her head into the room.

"Mommy, Mommy!" Rachel crooned. "Guess what?! I got a friend to play with! His name is Rider, and you can't see him cuz he's imvisbul but he can play with me! And we're playing house and he can be the daddy!"

Rachel's eyes sparkled with such happiness, her mother couldn't help but smile. Before she could respond, Rachel was chattering away with her new playmate. "I think Rachel has an imaginary friend," she whispered to her husband who had heard the commotion as well and was coming to investigate.

"Is that….normal?" he asked, concern etched across his features. "I mean, should we worry about this?" Robert Masterson loved his daughter but was completely oblivious when it came to children. As an only child who didn't get to watch a sibling grow up, he knew nothing about the stages kids went through on their path to adult-hood. His wife, Mary, was frequently exasperated by his ignorance of the needs of their daughter and would joke that he expected her to change her own diaper as soon as she could walk, eat steak for dinner as soon as she had teeth, and hit a home run as soon as she could hold a base-ball bat. He found their daughter's complete dependence on them a little frightening and wondered occasionally if his incompetence was as glaringly obvious to others as it was to him.

"It's fine, Rob, perfectly normal for a child her age, especially since she plays by herself so much. It's kinda cute, don't you think, how she made him up all by herself?"

He actually thought it was a little weird, how she looked like she was talking to herself, but his wife wasn't worried, and Rachel seemed happy and content, and just maybe this would give him a little reprieve from her constant requests to "play with me, Daddy!" which was cute and endearing, but kind of annoying when all he really wanted to do was watch the game. Satisfied with his conclusions, Rob closed the door on his daughter and her new "friend" and shuffled happily into the kitchen to get a snack.

Chapter Three

Favorite hot pink tee shirt with the unicorn on the front? Check. Ruffled purple skirt? Check. Brand new sparkly sneakers? Check. Little Mermaid backpack, lunchbox, and matching umbrella, just in case it rains? Check, check, and double check! Rachel took inventory as she got herself ready for her first day of school.

"We are ready for kinnergarden, Rider!" Rachel declared as she checked herself out in the mirror one last time. "I can't wait to go to school! There's gonna be lots of kids there, and a big playground with a super tall slide – I know cuz I saw it when Mommy drove by there; and I bet we get to learn all kinds of cool things like how to read so we can read as many stories as we want and we won't have to wait for Mommy to read 'em to us! And I hope our teacher is nice, don't you? I bet she's pretty, too, like the Sunday school teacher!"

"Rachel, time to go, sweetie!" Mary Masterson called, as she searched through her giant hobo bag, looking for her keys. "We don't want to be late on your first day!" In desperation, she dumped the entire thing out onto the counter. A baggie full of Cheerios, a Barbie doll head, 3 barrettes, and a overripe, half-eaten banana tumbled out along with five tubes of lipstick, her wallet, and mercifully, her keys. Her eyes scanned the mess she had just made then traveled around the rest of the room taking in the sink full of dishes, the fingerprints on the windows, and the My Little Ponies scattered across the carpet. She was definitely ready to have a few hours to herself every day. Although she could hardly bear the thought of being away from her daughter, the chance to tidy the house in peace and maybe even sneak in a phone call to her best friend or take a long, relaxing, bubble bath without interruption was a fantasy only a mother could appreciate.

Rachel trotted happily into the kitchen and grabbed one of the barrettes off the counter. Sticking it haphazardly into her hair, she grabbed her mother by the sleeve and dragged her out the door, chattering excitedly. "Rider's afraid I won't want to play with him anymore if I make new friends at kinnergarden, but I told him that's silly, cuz he's my best friend! I just hope the other kids are nice to me like Rider is, not like that mean boy at the playground that pushed me off the swing!"

"Sweetie," Mary said cautiously, hoping she wouldn't spoil her daughter's first-day enthusiasm but worried her obsession with her imaginary friend might ostracize her, "you know, if you make some real friends at school, maybe you won't need to play with Rider anymore. And I'm sure they'll be nice to you, honey, but maybe you shouldn't talk about Rider with your new friends, because

Kellie McAllen

they can't talk to him like you do."

"Rider is a real friend, Mommy! And they can too talk to him; he can hear just fine. Can't you, Rider? He says yes, Mommy, he can hear everything I can hear."

"But sweetie, they can't hear Rider, and they can't see him either, and I'm afraid they might tease you if they think you're talking to yourself. You can still talk to Rider at home. I just think it would be better if you didn't talk about him at school. Do you understand?"

Rachel didn't really understand why she shouldn't talk about Rider, but she didn't want to be teased, so she nodded her head and promised her mother she'd do her very best to keep Rider a secret.

* * * * * * *

As the Masterson family van joined the throng of similar vehicles weaving though the crowded parking lot of Allendale Elementary, Rider's tension grew. He did not share Rachel's enthusiasm towards kindergarten even a little. He knew school meant a whole new world for Rachel, full of exciting adventures, for sure, but also full of new people — children who would compete with him for Rachel's attention and grown-ups who would repudiate his existence altogether. Rachel was his whole world, and he didn't want to share her.

He saw the school rise up before her eyes, huge and looming, with hordes of laughing, talking children vying for her attention. Her hands were moist as she tucked one into her mother's and clutched tighter at the handle of her plastic pink lunchbox with the other. Mrs. Masterson squeezed Rachel's fingers and started chattering away about the bright classrooms full of colorful toys and games and the happy-looking teachers smiling welcomingly at the children funneling into their classrooms. She followed a garden of paper flowers taped to the wall that led to the kindergarten room, the petals of each surrounding a snapshot of a new student whose name was written in perfect penmanship down the stem. They found Rachel's between Paige and Samantha. Rider looked in vain for his own name among the blooms, not really expecting it, but hopeful all the same.

Miss Lindley stood at the door to their classroom, and her long blond hair, short flowery dress and perky smile gave away her new teacher naiveté. She bent down to tousle Rachel's hair as she welcomed them by name and then led them to the cubbies where Rachel could stow her Little Mermaid accoutrement. Her desk was nearby, with an alphabet-lined name tag marking her spot. Mary hugged her daughter goodbye, reminded her to listen and behave, then walked backwards out of the room, waving and blowing kisses till she was finally gone.

"Rider, I'm scared!" Rachel whispered under her breath as soon as her mother was out of sight. "I wish Mommy could stay, don't you?" Her fingered played nervously with the pencil box she had brought to her desk and she looked around in awe at the class full of children, some running and playing, others cowering in their seats. She recognized the plastic kitchen in the corner of the room like the one she had at home, but a group of kids were already using the matching table and dishes for a make-believe meal.

"Don't worry, Rachie, I'm here with you," Rider reassured her, always her most devoted advocate, even when his own fears left him wracked with worry.

Miss Lindley led another little girl to the desk in front of Rachel, and Rachel watched as she said her good-byes to her mother then looked around the classroom, fear etched on her face. "Hi," she stammered as her eyes met Rachel's, "I'm Paige."

Rachel smiled as she took in Paige's ruffled pink skirt and sparkly tennis shoes. In her hands was a pencil pouch with a unicorn galloping across a field of glitter, and her curly black hair was held in place by a Little Mermaid bow. "My name's Rachel," she replied, "I like your pencil box!"

Chapter Four

"Race you to the swings!" Rachel hollered as the school doors opened and the stream of kindergarteners was let loose on the playground. Despite modern concerns about the safety of playground equipment, Allendale Elementary offered all the old-fashioned fun a kid could ever want: a blistering-hot metal slide that was taller than the school itself, a row of butt-squeezing swings on finger-pinching metal chains, and right in the middle, a squeaky merry-go-round manned by the muscular 5th graders who slung screaming children around in a circle till they got dizzy and tumbled off.

"You always want to swing during recess!" Paige complained, panting to keep up with her friend and get to the swings before someone else took them. "Let's play on the merry-go-round instead!"

"No way, uh uh, I can't play on that crazy thing!"

"Why not? It's fun! Especially if one of the big kids pushes! You go so fast you almost fall off!" Paige grabbed

Rachel's arm and dragged her towards her favorite plaything.

Panicked, Rachel dug her feet into the ground and her eyes started to water, "I don't want to almost fall off, that's why! It's scary, and I don't like it, and neither does Rider!"

"Okay, don't cry, Rachel! We don't have to go on it! I didn't know it scared you so bad." Paige rushed back to comfort her friend whose terror was evident in her quivering voice. Paige's arms embraced her as the two sunk to the ground.

"My daddy pushed me on that one time and my stomach hurt so bad I barfed," Rachel whimpered. "And it made my head hurt, too. Mommy says they're dangerous and made Daddy promise not to push me on it anymore after that." Her breath hitched as she spoke, and tears threatened to spill from her eyes.

"Sshhh, it's okay," Paige whispered as she smoothed Rachel's hair and rubbed her back. Slowly, Rachel's breathing returned to normal, and her sniffles ceased.

"So who's Rider?" Paige asked when her friend had calmed enough to talk again. "You never talked about him before."

"He's….just a…….friend." Rachel desperately wished she hadn't mentioned her secret companion. Paige was curious and persistent and completely incapable of keeping her mouth shut.

"Does he live near you? Why doesn't he go to school with us?"

"He does go to school with us, I mean, sort of..." Rachel sputtered, her composure beginning to falter.

"Is he in a different grade? How come I never met him? Why doesn't he play with you at recess?" Paige babbled, skipping back toward the swing set, oblivious to Rachel's hesitance.

Lagging behind, torn between wanting to share her secret with her friend and her mother's admonishment not to, Rachel debated whether or not her new friendship could withstand her confession. Finally sensing Rachel's reticence, Paige halted and gave her friend a confused but encouraging look.

Rachel's desire to confide finally outweighing her worry, she whispered shakily, "Can you keep a secret?"

Rider's thoughts grew frantic as he considered the possible outcome of Rachel's revelation. Could someone actually believe in him, if their mind was young and open enough, not jaded and cynical like most of the grownups he knew?

Paige's face lit up with a smile as she bounced back to her friend's side. "I promise I'll never tell anybody!" she squealed, delighted by the thought of a surprise. Paige thrilled at the idea of knowing somebody's secret and she wished she had one of her own to divulge. Secrets were big-kid stuff, something her older sister constantly denied her, even though she crossed her heart and hoped to die.

"Rider's... special," Rachel whispered, unsure how to describe her unique relationship with the boy who lived inside her mind. "Nobody can see him, or hear him, but I can, and we've been friends for a really long time."

"So he's an imaginary friend." Paige nodded in understanding. "I had one of those once. His name was Seymour. But my sister told me only babies have imaginary friends, so I quit playing with him. Real friends are more fun anyway. But it's okay if you still have one!" she back-pedaled, eye widening in regret, hoping she hadn't offended her friend. Rider's heart plummeted at the thought that Rachel's new friend would never accept him. Someday, would Rachel stop believing in him too?

"He's not imaginary, he's real! I didn't make him up. He's always been there and he really talks to me. He's fun, and nice, and he's my best friend....besides you, I mean, and everybody thinks he's imaginary but he's not! Mommy told me not to talk about him — she said people wouldn't believe me." Rachel hung her head, digging her sparkly tennis shoe into the ground, her eyes threatening to tear again.

"I believe you, Rachie, I do! I just never heard of that before. But if you say it's true, then it must be." Paige's eyes twinkled, and a smile began to pull at the edges of her mouth as she contemplated the idea of a real live invisible boy. How could she possibly keep from spilling such an exciting secret?! She already wanted to tell everybody about Rachel's special friend.

"You can't tell anybody, Paige! I mean it!" Rachel demanded. She could already see the excitement bubbling up in Paige's eyes. "Nobody is going to believe you, and Mommy said everybody will make fun of me if they know about it! You have to keep this just between us, okay?"

"All right, I promise not to tell anybody, but you have to tell me all about him! Wait, is he here now? Can he see me? Can he hear me? Can he talk to me? Hi, Rider! Where are you?" Paige looked around for some kind of sign of Rider's presence — a shimmer in the air perhaps. Her hands probed the space around them, searching for substance, an invisible body she could feel but not see.

"It's not like that, Paige." Rachel lowered her voice to the barest of whispers and looking around furtively to make sure no one was witness to the story she was about to tell.

"He doesn't have a body at all, not even an invisible one. It's like, he lives inside me, in my head or something. If I can see something, so can he. And he can talk to me, but you can't hear it cuz he says it inside my head, ya know?"

"So he can hear me?"

"Yes, and he says hello, and he's pleased to meet you, and he thinks you're fun and nice and he's glad you're my friend." Rachel giggled. "And he likes your hair!"

Paige patted her unruly curls and smiled happily, pleased to have an admirer. "What else does he think about me?"

"He's excited that somebody believes that he's real, and he's happy to have somebody new to talk to, and he's worried that you're going to spill the beans cuz you have a big mouth!" Rachel was giddy with pleasure at the success of her revelation.

"Rider! That was not a very nice thing to say, even if it is kinda true, but I promise I won't tell anybody, especially not my stupid sister who never tells me any of her secrets!" Paige declared, as she slung her arm around her best friend, and her new acquaintance, and led them both to the swings.

Chapter Five

Show and Tell was everybody's favorite part of Mondays in Mrs. Miller's 2nd grade class. Mrs. Miller was clever enough to realize that having something to look forward to on Mondays would make coming back to school after the weekend a lot more enjoyable, so she started every week with a rousing episode of Show and Tell. It was actually more like Brag and Outdo, as the students tried everything in their power to impress their classmates and upstage the kid before them, getting downright outrageous in their presentations. Macie Stewart always had the newest Barbie doll accessory like the hot pink convertible or the ginormous dream house so big she had to have her brother lug it into the classroom one day, and Lance Keller always brought in some kind of video game that no one else cared about, but he would go on and on about how he had beaten the 3-headed dragon on level 7 in record time. Then there was Paige, whose stories of weekend adventures to exciting places like Chicago and Mackinac Island blurred the lines between reality and fantasy. The adventures she described became so fantastic that the class began to doubt she had been anywhere at all and accused her of fabricating the entire tale.

Rachel should have guessed her relationship with Paige would predispose her classmates towards skepticism when she decided to share her incredible secret, but in her naivety, she couldn't imagine the cruel reaction her classmates would have to her unbelievable story. Rachel's knees bounced nervously under her desk as she anxiously awaited her turn at the front of the classroom. Currently, Paige had the spotlight and was reminiscing about last weekend's trip to Cedar Point, the "World's Best Amusement Park," or so Paige said. She was bragging about the sheer number of massive roller coasters there and vividly describing those she had been brave enough to ride. Nobody was buying her story because they all knew that she was barely tall enough to go on the kiddie coasters. She was a great storyteller, though, and she described the sensation of losing your lunch while hanging upside down from the top of the coaster with details so realistic that Rachel started to feel a little queasy herself.

Finally, it was Rachel's turn, and the room grew silent as she marched to the front of the class, her face a mask of seriousness as she steeled herself to share her deepest secret. Rider had been warning her all morning that this was a bad idea, but she had resolutely ignored him, convinced that her peers would believe her if only she could make them understand. She turned to face her classmates and took a deep breath before launching into her confession. "Today I want to tell you about my best friend, Rider," she declared, looking bravely into their eyes. When she began to explain to them about the boy who lived inside her, who talked to her and told her funny jokes and kept her company so she was never alone, her classmates responded exactly how Rider had feared.

"That's stupid!" Mason Jordan, the class bully, said loudly, laughing at Rachel and sparking similar reactions from her other classmates. "Rachel's such a baby she actually believes her imaginary friend is real! What a loser!" The others began snickering and whispering desultory comments about Rachel to each other. Their voices grew louder and louder, the cacophony threatening to overtake her as Rachel's hopes plummeted.

"I'm not a baby and he's not imaginary! Rider's real! As real as anybody!" Rachel begged them to understand, but their taunts only grew the more she insisted.

"Cra-zy, Cra-zy, Cra-zy!" chanted Mason, followed by the others, pounding their fists on their desks in rhythm with their taunts.

"Quiet down!" Mrs. Miller demanded, rapping her knuckles on her desk, trying to regain control of her classroom. The taunts decreased in volume, but the children still giggled and whispered and wiggled excitedly in their chairs. "Rachel, that's enough! Don't you have enough sense to know better?" She snarled, grabbing Rachel by the collar and ushering her back to her desk. Mason stuck out his foot as Rachel walked by, and she stumbled into her chair, red-faced and teary-eyed. Mrs. Miller tried to take the attention off Rachel by focusing the class on checking their math assignment, but every time Rachel lifted her head, another classmate caught her eye and mouthed the word "crazy" at her, their twisted smiles tearing holes in

Soulmate

her fragile heart.

Despite the constant taunting from her classmates, Rachel held fast to her conviction that Rider was real, so much so that Mrs. Miller felt it necessary to hold a conference with Rachel's parents to get to the bottom of her delusion. Remembering the imaginary friend she used to talk about, the Mastersons blew it off as Rachel's attempt to garner attention, but they made it clear to Rachel that the nonsense had to stop. Rachel never mentioned it again in front of her parents or teachers but she never denied it to her classmates, and she quickly became the brunt of their jokes. They called her "Crazy Rachel" whenever the teacher couldn't hear them and they avoided her like the plague, claiming that, "the crazy would rub off." Rachel tried to convince herself she didn't care. She had Paige and Rider, and that was enough.

Chapter Six

"We're moving to Indianapolis!" Typically overdramatic like most 15 year olds, Rachel sobbed as she threw herself at her best friend, the only person she'd ever truly been close to besides Rider, the only person who believed in Rider's existence.

"What?! When?!" Paige gasped, dumbstruck by the possibility of losing Rachel and Rider, the only friends she'd ever needed, the only people she'd ever bothered to try to get to know. The three of them had been together from kindergarten, ever since Rachel told Paige her secret. Now the thought of separation was unfathomable, especially to Paige. Who would be friends with her if she didn't have Rachel and Rider? She had long ago alienated herself from all her classmates. Rachel and Rider were all the companionship she ever needed.

"Next week! Isn't it horrible?! In the middle of the school year! I can't believe my parents are doing this to me. It's for my dad's work. He'll lose his job if he doesn't take this transfer."

"That totally sucks! But what about me? At least you'll have Rider with you! I'm gonna be all alone in this cesspool of loneliness! Who's gonna hang out with me, huh?" Paige's tone was sarcastic, but her face revealed her anxiety.

"You totally suck! I have to go to a whole new school with all new people in a new city where I don't know anybody! And it's not exactly like having Rider around is gonna make me look like less of a chump sitting all by myself in the cafeteria! I'm sure all the kids will be like, 'Oh cool, this new girl talks to herself and acts like a weirdo, let's go make friends with her!' " Rachel wailed, tears threatening to spill from her eyes. After a moment, she noticed the dorky-looking kid whose locker was next to hers staring at her. "Yes, I know, I'm crazy!" she hollered at the gangly, pimply-faced boy who rolled his eyes as he slammed his locker and walked away, shaking his head. "Geez, even the losers think I'm a freak-show!" She buried her face in her hands and let the tears soak her palms.

"I'm sorry, Rach, I know it sucks for you." Paige wrapped her arms around Rachel's heaving shoulders. "This totally sucks for everybody. Rider, you're so lucky you don't have to worry about making friends and fitting in."

"Yeah, but I can't get away from the crazy one I already have!" Rider said, and Rachel giggled. He always knew how to lighten the mood.

"You don't even have to tell me." Paige held up her

hand. "I know exactly what that rotten little dweeb is saying! You know, I won't mind getting away from your constant insults, Rider!"

"He says he won't mind not having to look at your ugly mug all the time, either," Rachel replied, sticking out her tongue. Rider didn't have control over her body, but sometimes it was hard to tell if she was acting out her own desires, or his.

"Well, if you're leaving next week, then we just have to have an epic goodbye party this weekend! Let's do something fun like sneak into a night club or something!" Her eyes widened in excitement as she imagined a weekend wild enough to base another Hangover sequel on.

"Whoa, there, party girl, we have, like, a whole huge house to pack up this weekend. My mom's never gonna let me go out."

"Hmm, total bummer. I guess I'll just have to come help you so you get done faster! There will be pizza, won't there? And maybe some of those cookies your mom makes..."

"I'll see what I can do." Rachel smirked. "Are you actually going to help or are you just gonna hang around, eating and distracting me?"

"That's what I love about you, crazy girl — you know me so well!" Paige smiled and threw her arms around her best friend. The two embraced for what was probably a little longer than socially acceptable, but they never had cared much about social norms. As the bell rang, the girls

Soulmate

gave each other one last squeeze and headed off to their re-
spective classes, their hearts heavy with the devastating
news.

Chapter Seven

You can do this! Rachel told herself as she readied for her first day at her new school — combing her hair perfectly smooth, checking for lipstick on her teeth, and looking at her outfit from every angle to make sure it was perfect.

"You look beautiful, as always," Rider encouraged as Rachel checked her makeup one last time. She'd persuaded her mother to take her to the mall for new clothes, new gold highlights in her already-blonde hair, a manicure, a bottle of Bath & Body Works Sweet Pea body spray, and a new backpack to replace the grungy pink one she'd been carrying since 7th grade. Her mother had agreed out of guilt over the move, so Rachel was starting school looking cooler than she had ever felt. Unfortunately, her self-esteem was not quite as sparkling as her glittery lip gloss. Rider's compliments helped a little, but he was so free with them it was hard to know how true they really were. Not a day went by that Rider didn't tell her she was beautiful or brilliant or something equally wonderful. He acted like he meant it, though, and Rachel hoped his natural bias hadn't blinded him to her flaws. She just hoped he was valiant enough to warn her before she did something really lame or embarrassing.

"Rider, you know I love you, but I will not go all space cadet talking to you in front of other people today! Keep your comments to yourself, okay? I don't need you making me laugh in the middle of English class because you find something amusing to tell me." Rachel was actually a little excited at the prospect of starting over where no one knew her as weird or crazy. She doubted she could maintain the charade for long, but she was going to try.

"I can't help it if I'm incredibly witty and charming and the spotlight of attention!" Rider bragged, "Besides, who else am I supposed to talk to?"

"I know, but I don't want to look like a freak on the first day in a new school! So just chill, okay?" Rachel grabbed her backpack and headed to the kitchen to pack her lunch. She was terrified and thrilled at the same time about starting a whole new life in a new town with new people at a new school. This could finally be her chance to fit in for once, to be treated like a normal teenager, not like a freak known for talking to an imaginary friend her whole life. What she wasn't sure of was whether Rider was the only thing that made her a freak. Maybe she still wouldn't fit in. Maybe they would take one look at her and know right away she was a loser who wasn't worth a second glance. She tried not to think about it too much or it made her want to barf.

"What should I take, Rider? Is a PB&J too

juvenile? How about a ham sandwich? Definitely not those stupid tubes of yogurt. Yogurt should NOT be purple. Yuck. Do we have any crackers besides Goldfish? Seriously, you'd think I was four, the food Mom buys for me." Rachel jabbered nervously as she threw her lunch choices onto the counter. "Do we have any lunch bags, Mom?" she bellowed.

"Your lunch bag is in the cupboard next to the fridge, honey," her mother hollered back from the laundry room.

"I am not taking that stupid, polka dot lunch bag to my new school, Mom! Don't we have any plain bags?" she whined, rummaging through the cupboards. She didn't know where anything was in this new house.

"There's some Wal-Mart bags in the pantry you can use!"

"MOOOMMMM!!!! Please! Are you trying to humiliate me?!" Rachel threw all the food back into the fridge in frustration. "I'll just buy my lunch. Can I have five bucks?"

"Fine, you can check my wallet for some cash, but you're not buying lunch every day, you hear me? Who knows what they put in that cafeteria food. I'll buy you some paper bags if that's what you want so you can take some healthy food from home," Mrs. Masterson replied, coming in to the kitchen to check on her daughter.

"Oh, it's going to be okay, sweetheart," Mary took one look at her daughter's terrified face and came to embrace her. "You're going to be just fine at this new school, honey. How could you not be? You're so beautiful, and smart, and kind, and, well, everybody will love you, I promise!"

Rachel rolled her eyes and shook her head. "No Mom, they're not going to fall in love with me the minute I show up! Just because you think I'm wonderful doesn't mean anybody else does. I'll be lucky if anybody even talks to me." Rachel's complaints turned into sobs.

Mary smoothed her daughter's hair and dabbed under her eyes with a tissue. "Oh honey, I'm so sorry you have to go through this. What can I do to help?"

"Nothing, Mom, I just have to deal with this on my own. I've gotta go or I'll be late. I'll see you tonight." Wiping the tears from her face, she took one last glance at her reflection in the toaster and headed for the door.

Their new house was in a pretty big subdivision, so the odds were good that a lot of kids her age lived nearby, but she had been too busy unpacking and helping her parents put things away to go and scope out the neighborhood. The bus stop was at the end of her street, and as she walked towards it, she could already see a small crowd gathering.

"Make sure you introduce me," Rider teased as Rachel neared the group of students. Just then, the big yellow bus rumbled up to the corner and the door whooshed open.

"So much for introductory small talk," Rachel mumbled as she joined the end of the line of students filing onto the bus. As she entered, she scanned the rows frantically, trying to find a safe place to sit. Of course, there were no empty benches. Should I risk sitting next to a cute guy? Or try to find a friendly looking girl? Maybe I should pick a dweeb. They might be willing to talk to me. She felt the seconds ticking by as she considered her choices, and the bus driver was staring in irritation at her indecision.

"Pick a seat, missy," the driver barked just as Rachel gave up her searching and slumped into the first empty spot. The bus pulled away with a lurch that sent her bag tumbling down the aisle. Stumbling awkwardly to rescue it, she grabbed the bag and cradled it in her arms for safekeeping. Great first impression, she sighed, and dared to take a peek at the person next to her. The girl had unremarkable, shoulder-length brown hair, a forgettable set of facial features, and an utterly ordinary outfit composed of off-brand jeans and a plain blue tee shirt. She wore no makeup, and there was nothing particularly attractive about her, but her broad smile was the best thing Rachel had seen all day.

"First day?" she asked, as she peered knowingly at Rachel, taking in her lace cami and cropped leather jacket, designer skinny jeans, and buffed leather riding boots. "I'm Tara. I don't think I've seen you before, and you look like you're freaked out, so I figure you must be new. Must not know anybody, either, since you sat next to me. Not that I bite or anything, but you wouldn't know it by the way everyone avoids me. I'm happy to be friends with you, but I'm warning you, it's probably social suicide, and you look like you just might be cool enough to fit in okay... if you stay away from the likes of me." Rachel's mouth dropped open and she stared at Tara. What was up with this girl? Who talks like that about themselves?

"I like her!" Rider said, intrigued by her candor. "I bet you could even tell her about me and she'd be cool with it." His mind perked at the idea of finding another human who could believe in him. He was already missing Paige.

"She just admitted she's a spaz, Rider! I'm trying to fit in here, not sign up for loser club!"

"Oh yeah, like you were SO cool back in Allendale!"

"I know I wasn't cool, dorkface, and it was because of you! I'm trying to change my image here!"

"Uh, are you okay? Your face is kinda scrunched up weird. You look like you're in pain.....or about to have a bowel movement," Tara asked, giving Rachel a quizzical look, but still managing to seem friendly despite the sarcasm.

"Sorry, I'm just....I'm kind of......stressed, I guess." Rachel grimaced. It was always a little challenging to look normal while she and Rider had conversations in her head. "My name's Rachel and we just moved here from Michigan. And no, I don't know a soul, which is....kind of....unnerving." She gave Tara a quick smile in return, and then tried surreptitiously to scan the rest of the bus to see if anyone was looking at her. The girls in the seat next to them looked like freshmen, still small and immature, looking through a Tiger Beat magazine together and oohing over the pictures of cute boys. Behind them was an enormous hillbilly with headphones in his ears and a filthy ball cap shielding his eyes. Rachel couldn't think of a casual way to turn around and look at the seat behind her, but she could hear two boys talking about their favorite race car drivers, and they didn't sound cool, so she hoped they weren't.

"Have you got your schedule yet? Maybe we have a class together," Tara said, still holding out an olive branch.

"Um, yeah, I think I have Chemistry first period." Rachel dug in her bag for her schedule. "Then World History, World Literature, followed by lunch then Algebra 2, Art, and PE — your basic misery list." She showed the offending paper to Tara who nodded in sympathy.

"We actually have 3rd period together. Mrs. Warneki is pretty cool for a teacher. We're reading *The Lord of the Flies* right now. Have you read it?"

"We were reading it at my old school, so I guess at least I won't be too behind in that class. Kind of weird how they want us to read about kids killing each other, isn't it?"

"I think it's an allegory for the social hierarchy of high school, actually, so it's pretty apropos in that regard," Tara replied, excited to be discussing literature with another student, even if they did have different opinions.

"Well, I don't need to be Ralph, just as long as I'm not Piggy."

Tara laughed at Rachel's astute declaration, and the

two grabbed their bags and stood up as the bus rolled into the parking lot. "Come on, I'll show you the way to your first class, at least," Tara offered as the pair exited the bus and made their way into the school. "What's your locker number? I'll help you find that, too. Then you're on your own, at least till 3rd period."

"231. Do you know where that's at?" Rachel scanned the crowded parking lot and the horde of students milling around the front of the school. Rap music thumped from one of the cars behind her and the air smelled like cigarette smoke and Axe body spray.

"Sure. It's right by room 230, which just so happens to be your chemistry class, so that's some luck. But it's like a mile away from most of your other classes, so... sucks to be you, I guess."

"Story of my life," Rachel muttered, climbing the stairs to the second floor. This school was a lot bigger than Allendale High, Rachel realized. She was going to be getting plenty of exercise climbing these stairs a dozen times a day to get to her locker. Maybe she'd just schlepp all her books around in her bag instead.

"Well, here you go, locker 231. If it sticks, just kick it; that usually works. I've gotta bolt because my locker's way far away. See you in Lit class!" Tara grinned and waved as she trotted off.

Rachel dug her locker combination out of her pocket and carefully turned the knob to all the right numbers, but the door didn't budge. She tried jiggling the handle and bumping it with her hip with no success before finally hiking up her leg and giving it a good whack with the heel of her boot. The door rattled, but stay firmly shut. Looking around in desperation, hoping that by some miracle a maintenance man was nearby, Rachel's eyes landed on a tan, angular face topped with sandy blond waves. Bright green eyes and a smirk told her he had been enjoying her conundrum.

"Need some help?" Green Eyes offered, dropping his bag on the ground next to hers and reaching towards her locker. "You have to pull up on the handle, then jiggle it loose, then kick it if it needs it," he offered, demonstrating his technique. The locker door swung open with ease and Green Eyes shouldered his bag and saluted before sauntering away.

"Who was that masked man?" Rachel quipped, hanging her backpack in her locker and pulling out a notebook and pencil.

"Green Eyes? That's what you're calling him? Why not Tall, Dark and Handsome?"

"He didn't exactly tell me his name, now did he?" Rachel rolled her eyes but secretly appreciated Rider's teasing. His sense of humor relieved some of her stress. "At least he offered to help me. Otherwise I'd still be kicking at that stupid locker! Be glad somebody was nice to me, otherwise you'd have to listen to me complaining all day."

"Better than watching you ogle some green-eyed hottie!"

"You think he's a hottie? Geez, Rider, I didn't

know that was your type!" Rachel joked, the repartee brightening her face as she entered the classroom. Taking the first empty seat she saw, Rachel nodded to the girl next to her, a leggy brunette with too much eye makeup on, and got a scowl in response. "Note to self, don't nod at the natives."

The teacher handed her a textbook and introduced her to the class as Rebecca from Minnesota, but didn't give her a chance to correct him before starting in on his lecture. An hour later the cycle repeated, only this time the teacher got her name right ,and Rachel didn't bother to nod at anybody, so nobody scowled. By 3rd period, her heart was as heavy from the indifference of her peers as her arms from carrying all her textbooks to the far end of the school. She was thrilled to see Tara in the back of the class, waving and pointing at the empty desk next to her.

"So how's your first day going?" Tara's voice was a happy chirp.

Rachel slumped into the desk, plopping her heavy pile of books on top of it. "Stellar. A cute guy helped me get my locker open, but otherwise I've been the invisible girl. So far you're the only one who's actually talked to me."

"Sorry. The students here are, shall we say, a little self-absorbed? Maybe if you try out for a sport or join a club or something. Of course, what do I know; I'm not exactly Miss Popular, so clearly I'm not the one to give advice on how to fit in around here."

"Don't you have any friends?" Rachel blurted, then

realized how rude that sounded. So far, Tara was the only person who'd even bothered to introduce ~~herself.~~

"Oh sure, I'm not a loner or anything. I have lots of friends in science club." Tara seemed nonplussed by the accidental insult. "You're welcome to sit with us at lunch if you want."

Rachel doubted the science club was where she'd make friends, but it was better than sitting alone, so after World Lit was over, she followed Tara to the cafeteria, purchased a plate of mystery meat, and took a seat with the science geeks.

"This is Rachel," Tara announced to the motley group of teens, "She's new. Rachel this is Reggie, Eve, Tyler, and Garrett." She introduced the group with a wave of her hand, leaving it up to Rachel to figure out who was who. The group murmured a greeting in response and made room for her at the table.

"So who's your favorite doctor?" asked a skinny Asian boy with straight, dark hair that hung over his eyes and a tee shirt with what looked like a blue phone booth on it.

Puzzled, Rachel shrugged. "I just moved here, I don't have a doctor yet." Laughter erupted around her and Rachel blushed in embarrassment, unsure of her faux pas.

"Dude, she don't watch no Doctor Who! Look at her! She probably watch them weddin' shows or somethin'!" smirked the enormous black boy with fists as big as melons and neon sneakers the size of clown shoes.

"Oh yeah, you're one to judge stereotypes, Reggie," taunted Eve, a tall redhead with a face full of freckles and the palest skin Rachel had ever seen. "You look like a line-backer but you cry at ASPCA commercials!"

Reggie's face twisted into a mask of sympathy. "Them mangled-lookin' puppies are sad, and that Sarah McLachlan song'll make anybody cry!"

"Now these are my people!" Rider cheered, enjoying the good-natured ribbing. Rachel felt her spirit lift for the first time in weeks as she listened to their easy cama-raderie. She didn't know how well she fit in with them, but at least they didn't seem to mind her presence.

"I'm Tyler." A short but otherwise attractive boy with curly brown hair and dimples held out his hand to Rachel. Tara's eyes followed his hand and Rachel could sense Tara's attraction. Rachel definitely didn't want to make her new friend jealous, so she quickly dropped Tyler's hand and turned to Eve.

"I love your hair," she said, lightly brushing the coppery locks. Eve smiled and ran her fingers through her hair self-consciously.

"We're going to the theater tonight to see the new Batman movie if you want to come. It starts at 7 at the Multiplex."

"Say yes, say yes, say yes!" Rider pleaded. "You know I want to see that."

"Thanks, I'll ask when I get home." She wasn't too interested in Batman, but a movie night sounded fun, and the science geeks didn't seem too bad after all.

The conversation turned to more science-y things, and Rachel got a little lost in the mumbo-jumbo, but at least it was better sitting alone.

"Anybody going to algebra next?" Rachel asked as the lunch bell rang. "I have Mr. Volnar in room 201."

"Ugggghhh!" came a chorus of replies. Clearly she was in for a special kind of math torture if this crowd thought it was bad.

"My class is next door, so I'll show you the way," offered Garrett, the Doctor Who aficionado. Rachel thought she had the school layout pretty much figured out, but she appreciated the company, so she nodded gratefully, dumped her trash and followed Garrett out of the cafeteria.

"I'm not just a Doctor Who fan, I'm also into anime and cosplay!" He jabbered on about his strange collection of interests as Rachel nodded absentmindedly, not understanding most of the words he was saying. "Well, here you are," Garrett announced as they approached her algebra room, "Don't try talking in this class. Mr. Volnar doesn't like the sound of anyone's voice but his own. Soreja mata!" Rachel waved goodbye to her kooky new friend and steeled herself for a miserable hour.

"Got a boyfriend already?" a husky voice whispered in Rachel's ear, and she turned to find Green Eyes grinning at her.

"No! I, uh, he's, uh…we just met…" Rachel stammered as her handsome helper slipped past her with a smirk and took a seat in the back of the class next to the leggy brunette from 1st period. The only other open seat was in the front row, so Rachel plopped her notebook down with a huff and glanced back to see Green Eyes engaged in an intimate tête-à-tête with the scowler.

Mr. Volnar proved to be as boring as he was egocentric, and the hour seemed interminable. Rachel wanted desperately to turn around and see what the mystery boy was doing, but she kept her head turned towards the front and her mouth shut instead and wished for the period to end. Rider took the opportunity to amuse her by cracking jokes about Mr. Volnar's polyester pants, his cowlick, and his aviator style eyeglasses, and he almost sent her into hysterics when the teacher stuck his hand in the back of his pants instead of his back pocket.

Despite Rider's best efforts, Algebra eventually ended without any embarrassing mishaps, and Rachel was happy to see Reggie in her art class and Tyler in P.E. Tara saved her a seat on the bus ride home, so all together the day was not nearly as miserable as Rachel had imagined. Her new friends were not exactly the hipsters she was hoping to meet, but at least she wasn't completely ignored. Grabbing a snack from the kitchen, Rachel headed to her room and started in on her homework, hoping her mom would be impressed enough to reward her with a movie night.

Chapter Eight

"Hi, honey, how was school?" Mary poked her head into Rachel's room with a hopeful smile. Sharing Rachel's golden hair and trim figure, Mary Masterson looked younger than her 40 years, but she was all mom on the inside.

"It was okay." Rachel shrugged. "I got invited to the movies tonight. Could you give me a ride?" she begged, unleashing the power of her puppy dog eyes.

"Mmhmm, and I suppose you need $20 bucks for a ticket and popcorn, too?"

"Please?" Rachel grinned back, slapping her palms together and pouting her bottom lip.

"IF you get your homework done first," Mary demanded, and Rachel nodded excitedly.

"Already did it. Can we go soon? There might be a

Soulmate

line — it's opening night."

"What movie are you seeing?"

"Ahh, the new Batman?" Rachel replied hesitantly, hoping her mother wouldn't be too curious about her daughter's sudden interest in Sci-Fi.

"Since when do you like Batman?" There wasn't much that escaped her attention.

"It's supposed to be really good," Rachel offered limply.

Mary propped a hand on her hip and raised an eyebrow. "Who exactly is going to this movie with you, young lady? You do not have permission to be dating just yet, especially someone we don't even know."

"Tell her you've got a date with three hot boys all at the same time!" Rider teased.

"It not a date, Mom," Rachel sighed, ignoring Rider, "It's a group of kids I met at school today. They're... into that kind of thing. I just wanted to hang out with them."

"Okay, I suppose. But I'm picking you up right after the movie. It is a school night, you know."

"Thanks, Mom!" Rachel squealed, and jumped up to give her mom a hug.

* * * * * * *

The lobby was crowded with boys in Batman tee

48

shirts and black masks as Rachel struggled through the horde looking for a familiar face. A glimpse of bright orange hair caught her eye and she headed towards it, sure it had to be Eve. Suddenly, an eager face popped up in front of her and Rachel gasped in surprise.

"I already bought your ticket for you, just in case they sold out. Reggie's saving us some seats," said a high-pitched voice from behind a vinyl Batman mask. The masked man, presumably Garrett, grabbed Rachel by the hand and led her the rest of the way to where Eve, Tara, and Tyler were gathered.

"This is gonna be the best version ever!" Garrett thrust his fist in the air with a whoop that sent him tumbling into the people behind him. They gave him a dirty look and a wider berth.

"Somebody give that kid some Ritalin – he's a menace to society," Rider griped, and Rachel chuckled under her breath.

Rachel was greeted with a chorus of hellos as she approached the circle, and she was offered popcorn from three different buckets as someone else stuck a Coke in her hand.

"Wow, guys, you didn't have to pay for everything. I brought money." She pulled some cash from her pocket. "How much do I owe you?"

"Your money's no good here," uttered Tyler in his best deep gangster voice. "Seriously, it's our treat tonight, since you're new and all," he said, returning to his natural pitch, a wide smile lighting up his face.

"That's…really awesome. Thanks, you guys." Rachel beamed, in awe of her new friends' generous welcome.

"It's nothing!" Tara laced her arm through Rachel's and headed towards the entrance to their theater. They spotted Reggie almost immediately, sitting in the middle of the front row with his long arms spread out on either side, saving enough seats for all of them. After several minutes of seat-swapping and arguing over who should sit where, it was decided that Rachel would sit between Tara and Eve with Tyler next to Tara and Reggie and Garrett on the other side. Garrett seemed a little disappointed to be so far away from Rachel, but the loud, dramatic previews soon distracted him and his attention was caught up in the trailer for the newest Superman movie coming soon to a theater near you.

As the plot waned and the soda and popcorn supply dwindled, Rachel decided to make a trip to the lobby for re-fills. Her attempts to carry three cups and two popcorn buckets seemed perilous, so Tyler took some from her hands and followed her out of the theater. Tyler offered to stand in line while Rachel used the bathroom, so she loaded up his arms with containers and gratefully dashed to the ladies' room. Fortunately, the bathroom was empty, so Rachel made it back before he had progressed to the front of the line.

"Here, I'll take over so you can go," Rachel offered, taking the empty cups and balancing them under her arms. Tyler winked and chucked her under the chin as he promised to be back in a flash.

"Looks like your date's a big eater," a familiar husky voice chuckled in Rachel's ear. "Did you dump the scrawny guy already?"

A rush of heat flooded Rachel's cheeks as she recognized the sexy purr of her mystery acquaintance. Her attraction was quickly replaced by annoyance. "Who are you and why do you insist on antagonizing me?"

Immediately embarrassed by her outburst, Rachel lowered her voice and amended, "I mean, you could at least introduce yourself if you're going to continue to provide commentary on my life."

"My apologies," Green Eyes replied with a chivalrous bow. "My name is Jason Decatur and I am pleased to make your acquaintance, Miss...?" He held out his palm like a gentleman and brought her hand to his lips for a quick kiss. An acerbic smile lit up his face when she obliged.

Rachel smiled and tried her best to curtsy without dropping all the cups and buckets. "Miss Masterson of Allendale, Michigan, but you may call me Rachel."

"Please, let me assist you!" Jason quickly offered, taking most of the containers.

"I've got it," said Tyler, grabbing the cups from Jason's arms with a glare. "She's with me."

Rachel frowned at Tyler's possessiveness. She was

definitely not going to infringe on Tara's crush (that was completely against girl code) and besides, she was more interested in Jason anyway. "I'm with a group of people," she corrected.

"Well, maybe next time you'll be with me," Jason proposed with a wink and a grin as he graciously bowed and retreated.

"Stay away from him, Rachel. He's bad news," Tyler warned, handing the buckets to the cashier for a refill with a scowl on his face.

"He seems really nice. He helped me get my locker open this morning," Rachel countered.

"Oh, he's charming, all right. That's how he got half the girls in the freshman class to go out with him. Don't fall for it, Rachel. There are plenty of other guys." A wistful smile graced his lips and he turned away quickly, busying himself with the popcorn and soda.

"I think you better stay away from that one, too," Rider declared, "Why the sudden interest from all these boys?" He knew, though, why the guys of Indy High were fawning over Rachel. She was beautiful inside and out, but she didn't know it, which made her all the more appealing. His presence had sullied her reputation up till now, and no one who knew her before could see her as anything but the strange girl who talked to her imaginary friend. But here in a new town, she was reborn, and no one could help but notice her loveliness. He was happy for her, sure, but he couldn't help but feel jealous.

Rachel and Tyler somehow managed to carry everything back to their seats where the fresh popcorn was eagerly claimed by their friends. Tyler smiled at Tara when he took his seat and her wariness dissolved as she took a sip from the drink in his hand and smiled back happily. Rachel never could quite get into the movie, so instead she let her mind wander. When her thoughts turned to boys, Rider entertained her by conjuring up a fantasy where every boy she met fell at her feet in awe and wonder and she couldn't move for the crowd of admirers surrounding her. She stifled a giggle when Rider imagined the boys piling on top of each other and toppling to their deaths as they grappled to be on top. She could always count on Rider to keep her company when she was bored.

When the movie ended, Rachel's new friends bid her goodnight, and she made her way outside where her mom's van was waiting at the curb. "I was going to park and come in so I could meet your friends, but I thought you might find that embarrassing," Mary teased.

"Yes, mother, that would be weird." Rachel rolled her eyes. "They're just a group of people who hang out together. They seem really nice."

"Well, I'm glad you made some friends already. I knew this move would be tough on you."

"It's not as bad as I thought it would be, actually. I think I might like it here," Rachel said musingly, her mind lingering on the kindness of her new friends and the sudden interest of the male population.

"Paige called the house tonight; I told her you went

to the movies. I hope she's doing okay. She seemed kind of sad."

Rachel took out her phone from her purse which had been on vibrate since school started and saw three missed calls and a dozen text messages from Paige. They grew in intensity until the last which was nothing but dozens of question marks and exclamation points. "Yikes, I think I better call her."

"Am I nothing to you now that you live in the big city?!" Paige screeched when she answered Rachel's call after half a ring. "I left you, like, a million messages!"

Rachel pulled the phone away to avoid bursting her eardrum. "I'm sorry, I'm sorry! I forgot to turn on my phone after school and then I went to the movies. My mom just told me you called."

"So who'd you go to the movies with?" Paige whimpered. "Did you already make new friends?"

"Just a group I met today. They're kinda geeky, but they were nice to me. I miss you! Who did you sit with at lunch today?" Rachel answered, trying to soothe her friend's nerves.

"No one! I chickened out and went to the library instead. Hannah Evers was there and we talked a little bit. She was working on an extra credit project," Paige explained with a hint of disdain. Hannah was the class nerd. She didn't really have any friends because she was always too busy being scholastic to notice anyone else. Rachel chuckled, imagining the scenario.

"So who are these people you're hanging with? Would I like them?" Paige asked, slightly calmer.

"I met this girl Tara on the bus and she introduced me to her friends. They're all in the.....science club," Rachel admitted sheepishly. "Everybody else pretty much ignored me today."

"Does Rider like them?" That was the great thing about Paige. She treated Rider like he was as real as anyone. She didn't ignore him just because she couldn't see him or hear him like some ignore the mentally handicapped, pretending they don't exist because they can't speak for themselves. She respected him and his opinions and she talked to him, which Rider loved more than anything.

"Yeah, he does actually."

"I'm happy for you then. I hope one of them is at least half as awesome as me, so Rider won't be lonely. Any cute boys in this group?"

"Yeah, so, I'm riding home with my mom," Rachel answered ambiguously, hoping Paige would get the idea. "I'll call you after school tomorrow, okay?"

"She really misses you, huh?" Mary said after Rachel ended the call. "You know, she's always welcome to visit anytime." Rachel appreciated the offer, but she knew it was unlikely that Paige's parents would drive four hours down and back just so she could see her friend. No, until one of them got a license and a car, phone calls would have to do.

Chapter Nine

The second day at a new school was a lot easier, Rachel thought as she carried her lunch bag to the table where the science club was sitting. Getting ready, picking a seat on the bus, and finding her classes today had all been a breeze compared with the anxiety of yesterday. She still felt a little like a spectacle, but in reality no one paid her any mind. She was nobody to most of the school. She figured she wasn't attractive enough to draw anyone's eye and hadn't done anything stupid enough to make a scene, so most people looked past her. Sitting with the science geeks might not earn her any popularity points, but at least they didn't completely ignore her. She definitely wasn't one of them, though, she thought, as their conversations swirled around her like a foreign language. Currently they were discussing a robotics competition coming up in March that they were hoping to win. Rachel couldn't figure out how to operate the can opener half the time, so she certainly wasn't going to be building any robots.

In algebra class, she found a seat a little farther back

than yesterday and looked around for Jason, but he wasn't there yet. He came rushing in with the bell and took the only seat left, which just happened to be right next to Rachel, but the twinkle in his eyes as he smiled at her made it clear that he was pleased with his luck. Mr. Volnar scowled at Jason's last-second arrival and began his lecture. To Rachel's surprise, Jason opened his notebook immediately and began writing.

What Volnar was saying didn't really seem noteworthy, so Rachel glanced nervously around the room at the other students to see if they too were diligently recording the lecture. To her relief, it appeared her classmates were just as uninterested as she was, judging by their blank stares and closed binders. When Mr. Volnar turned his back on the class to write on the chalkboard, his apathetic students seemed to slump further into their chairs. Jason quietly ripped a sheet of paper from his notebook and handed it to Rachel.

"Do you like '80s music?" the note asked, followed by an adorable drawing of a girl in spandex and leg warmers with big hair and a crop top that had the word "RADICAL!" scrawled across it. Rachel looked over to see Jason playing air guitar and head banging enthusiastically until the teacher started to turn around. Jason quickly dropped his charade and managed to look thoroughly engrossed in the lecture by the time Volnar had completed his turn, but Rachel was barely holding in her laughter, so she hid her red face behind her hand and faked a sneeze instead.

"Excuse me," she squeaked as Volnar turned his menacing stare towards her. Seemingly convinced by her cover-up, the teacher continued his monologue, and Rachel could see Jason writing again from the corner of her eye. Another note quickly appeared on her desk as soon as the teacher's attention returned to the blackboard.

"There's a concert at the park this Friday night. This 80's tribute band that's pretty good. Would you like to go?" he had scribbled in his tidy penmanship. Music notes dotted the corners of the page.

Rachel turned to see Jason wiggling his eyebrows and smiling eagerly as she nodded yes. He grabbed the paper back just as Mr. Volnar began another revolution, and this time Rachel managed to look studious and interested instead of bizarre. It was all she could do not to stare at Jason as he surreptitiously drew another picture on the page while still looking up at Mr. Volnar occasionally and acting like the perfect student. A few agonizing minutes later, the teacher turned around again, and Jason slipped her the note.

"I'll pick you up at 6:00 and take you to dinner first, unless you'd rather have a picnic in the park. Where do you live?" Rachel read, dumbfounded as she realized this was not just a casual invitation to a local event or even a group thing with him and his friends.

This was a date. A real - boy and girl alone - kind of date. Her first date. She tried really hard not to freak out that a totally hunky guy had just asked her to go out with him on her second day in a new school, for her very first ever real date, in algebra class of all places, but her self-control wasn't that great.

She realized she had a freakishly large grin on her face

and stars in her eyes, and she struggled to relax her expression before turning to glance at Jason. He was staring at her with anticipation, and she quickly nodded and offered him a small smile instead of the goofy one her mouth was trying to make.

"Uh, hello! Earth to Rachel! Come in Rachel!" Rachel finally heard Rider hollering as she floated back to earth on a happy little cloud of teenage bliss. He had been trying to get her attention for quite some time, if the edge to his voice was any indication.

"What, Rider? Can't you see I'm having a moment here?" Rachel thought with a touch of her own irritation evident.

"Sorry to burst your bubble, but you're not allowed to date yet, remember? And besides, Tyler warned you this guy was trouble. Look how fast he's making his move!"

"Did it ever occur to you that maybe he asked me out because he actually likes me, Rider? And that maybe Tyler said that because he's interested in me too and wants to eliminate the competition? Can't you just be happy for me that I'm finally making some friends?!" Rachel thought indignantly. She hoped Jason wouldn't see her annoyance and assume it was towards him.

"You already HAVE friends, Rachel – me and Paige, and the science geeks are cool, too. Why do you want some skirt-chasing playboy with smooth moves and a fake smile coming on to you?"

"You don't know anything about him, Rider! Now

Kellie McAllen

leave me alone so I can enjoy the moment! He's the first
guy who's ever asked me out. And he's gorgeous and funny and romantic, too. You're just jealous because I'm not
spending every second with you!"

Rider had always been her biggest supporter, so why
was he all of a sudden so averse to the idea of a guy paying
attention to her? She purposely tuned out Rider's reply and
started scribbling her response on the paper beneath the
picture he had drawn of a guy and a girl on a blanket with a
picnic basket between them.

"The picnic sounds nice. Can I meet you there
instead?" She wrote. She knew her parents would never go
for a boy picking her up, but she could probably convince
them to drop her off at the park for a concert with her new
"friends."

"Sure," Jason wrote back, "I'll get there early and
find us a great spot near the front."

Rachel smiled at him, and the grin he gave back
was enough to turn her insides into melted chocolate. She
wanted to look down to make sure it wasn't oozing out of
her, but she didn't want to break his gaze.

Rachel could sense that the hour was almost up by
the restlessness growing amongst her classmates, so she hid
the notes from Jason in her binder and tuned in to the
teacher to find out what the homework assignment was for
the evening.

"Where's your next class?" Jason asked when the

bell rang.

"Uh, I have art in room 123."

"Cool, I'm going that way, too." Jason dazzled her with another toothy smile and held out his hand, palm up.

Rachel wasn't sure what he wanted. Was he trying to hold hands? She stared at his hand awkwardly.

"Would you like me to carry your books?" he asked when he saw her confusion.

"Oh, sure. Thanks." Rachel handed over her books with a dazed grin, mesmerized by his piercing green eyes and the confident way he slid his fingers through his hair, musing it into casual perfection. They chatted as they strolled towards Rachel's art class, and Rachel was glad they were side by side instead of face to face. She wasn't sure she would be able to form coherent words if she was looking straight at him.

Rider was grumbling in the back of her head, but she did her best to ignore him, focusing instead on committing every word Jason said to memory so she could relive it later.

Reggie wasn't there yet, and Rachel wondered what he would say if he saw Rachel and Jason together. Did he share Tyler's negative opinion about Jason? She decided it was no one else's business who she dated, and she would keep the secret to herself for the time being, just in case someone might blab to her parents and ruin her first date before she even had it.

*   *   *   *   *   *   *

Rachel's mom was gone when Rachel got home from school, so she took the opportunity to call Paige who answered on the first ring, obviously desperate for some best-friend interaction. The two gossiped gleefully about all the new people Rachel had met so far and all those she'd left behind while Rachel pondered whether she should tell Paige about Jason.

On one hand, she knew that Paige would kill to have a guy like Jason ask her out and she didn't want to make her jealous, but Paige was her best friend and she was desperate to share her excitement with someone. As if sensing her secret, Paige prodded for more information about the cute boys at Rachel's new school, and Rachel finally gave in and spilled her juicy news.

"So there is this one guy who's pretty cute," Rachel said coyly, twisting a lock of hair around her finger. She was lying on her bed, propped up on her arms with her feet swinging in the air.

"If you're into that obviously perfect type," sniped Rider.

"Oh, really? And what is this cute guy's name?" Rachel could hear the curiosity in Paige's voice.

"Jason, but I... uh... I didn't know his name at first, so in my mind I called him Green Eyes because his eyes are this amazing shade of emerald. I don't say that out loud, of course!"

"Pukeface works for me."

"Ooo, a nickname already! So have you talked to him yet, or are you just admiring him from afar?" Paige teased.

"Yeah, we've talked a little bit. In algebra class.......when he asked me out," Rachel cooed.

"You mean when he passed you a note like a 3rd grader? It might as well have had a 'Do you like me?' checkbox!"

"Asked you out? Like, as in, a date? A real date?!" Paige's screech hit at all time high.

"If you call eating cold sandwiches and listening to bad music a date."

Rachel flopped over onto her back and kicked her shoes off. "Yep! This Friday. We're having a picnic in the park. Isn't that romantic?"

"Wow, that's amazing," Paige's voice was wistful. Apparently, everything about Rachel's new life was better than her old one. "So how does Rider feel about this? It's gotta be weird for him, dontcha think?"

"Rider is being a total pain in the you know what!" Rachel replied hastily then softened. "I think he's just jealous that I'm paying attention to someone other than him."

Rider snarled, but didn't respond. Could it be true that his misgivings stemmed from mere jealousy and not from some true apprehension about Jason's character?

"I guess I always kind of thought of Rider as your boyfriend, you know? I mean, I know it's not the same as a real live guy to go out with, but what you two have is, like, really special. Better even."

Rachel sighed. "Yeah, I get that. But I can't exactly marry Rider and have his babies, now can I? But Jason, now he would make pretty babies!"

Paige badgered Rachel for all the details about her upcoming date, and Rachel freely shared, glad to be able to talk about it to someone who seemed happy for her. Afterwards, Rachel sympathized with Paige about her inability to make friends with the kids she had known all her life but completely ignored. Sharing Tara's advice to her, Rachel suggested, "Maybe you should join a club or a sport or something?"

"Like what? Science club? I think that would do more damage than good to my popularity. And the only athletic talent I have is the ability to eat enormous amounts of junk food in one sitting!"

Rachel chuckled, imagining Paige with a vat of ice cream on her lap. "I know, I know. It was just a suggestion. Maybe you could talk your parents into letting you transfer. A fresh start, you know?" She'd never felt so responsible for someone else's troubles before.

"Right, like that'll happen." Rachel could hear Paige's eyeballs rolling around in her head. "I've gotta go, I've got some homework to do, but give Rider a hug for me and call me the minute you get home from that date! I want to hear every detail!"

Rachel blew her friend some air kisses and hung up, her heart a befuddled mix of happy and sad.

Chapter Ten

Paige's troubles temporarily forgotten, Rachel woke Wednesday morning with one thing on her mind: Jason Decatur. As she dressed, she wondered what his favorite color was and whether or not she looked good in it. Who doesn't like blue? She thought, and settled for a navy blouse that hugged her curves in all the right ways.

She wondered whether he would like the fragrance of her perfume or if she should skip it in case he was allergic and just rely on her deodorant and citrus-scented shampoo to keep her sweet-smelling. She compromised with one short burst down the front of her blouse, just enough to tantalize.

She kept her jewelry understated, too, with a pair of gold hoops and a letter "R" pendant hanging from a simple gold chain. She never did much with her long golden hair — it had a nice wave that looked good without a whole lot of work — but today she pinned a few pieces back to frame her face.

Rider was surprisingly quiet as she readied herself
for the day. Usually, he kept her laughing with bad jokes
and snide comments, but today all he'd done was compliment her hair and tell her to lay off the eye shadow. At
breakfast, he was so quiet the sound of her own chewing
became unbearable. "What's up with you today, Rider?"
she finally asked when she could stand the silence no
longer.

"Do you really want to 'have his babies'?" Rider
asked softly. She had admired other boys before, of course,
mostly movie stars and strangers she passed at the mall, but
it had never dawned on Rider that she might eventually fall
in love with one of them.

"Well, not right this minute!" Rachel laughed, but
the joke fell flat. "But someday maybe. I mean, he might
not be 'the one' but he is cute, and funny, and he seems really nice, so why shouldn't I go out with him?"

"I guess I just didn't realize you were looking for
'the one.' I thought I was your… soulmate."

Rachel let her spoon plop into her cereal bowl so
she could concentrate on the conversation. "Oh, Rider, I'll
never be as close to anybody as I am to you! You know I
love you, but, I'm human and I need to be with other hu-
mans sometimes, too."

"I get it. I'm not enough for you," Rider said and
closed himself off from the conversation.

"Rider, wait! You're being unfair! You can't really

expect me to spend my whole life with no one but you!"

"You mean like I have to do?" Rider thought to himself, his dreams disintegrating into ash, like paper set ablaze by the tiny spark of her declaration. He hadn't given much thought to the future, but it never crossed his mind that one day Rachel might want a partner other than him. Paige was easy to get along with; in fact it pleased him to no end that she believed in him and cared about him. So why did the thought of a male in Rachel's life make him so unhappy?

The two didn't speak to each other the rest of the morning, both plagued by guilt and self-righteous indignation at the same time. In an attempt to fill the void, Rachel struck up a lively conversation with Tara about the need for air fresheners on the bus, and her morning classes kept her busy enough she didn't have much time to think about the fact that Rider was not providing his usual witty commentary on her day.

In Literature class, Tara got called to the office a few minutes before the end of the period. She whispered to Rachel on her way out that she had a dentist appointment and would be back after lunch. When the bell rang, Rachel packed up her things slowly, in no hurry to have lunch without Tara. The science geeks were nice to her, but it seemed Tara was the only one who could carry on a "normal" conversation. As she approached her locker, she did a double take. A tall, hunky guy was blocking her way.

"Hi Jason," she stammered, "Isn't your locker down the next hall?" Real smooth, Rachel, she immediately thought. Now he's going to think I've been following him!

She hadn't, exactly, but she did happen to pay special attention every time she saw him.

"Yeah," he chuckled, presumably at the embarrassed look on her face. "But I was hoping I might be able to persuade you to eat lunch with me today." His lips turned up into a quirky smile, and he leaned casually against her locker as he awaited her response, clearly confident that she would accept.

Rachel's heart twisted in her throat as she realized Jason was really and truly interested in her. Never in her life had any of the boys at school showed her even the least bit of attention. In fact, they treated her and Paige like pariahs, afraid the girls' strangeness might detract from their own popularity if they even acknowledged their existence. Rachel was used to being ignored, and sometimes ridiculed, but sought out? Now that was a new one.

Rider desperately wanted to make a sarcastic comment about Jason's Ken Doll physique, his Ralph Lauren wardrobe, or his cocky GQ smile, but he could sense Rachel's pleasure at the unexpected attention, so he decided to hold his tongue and let her enjoy the moment. More than anything, he wanted her to be happy, and if Jason made her happy, well then he would just have to learn to like him, too. It had worked out okay with Paige; in fact, he relished their friendship, so maybe he could find a way to appreciate Jason.

It might even be fun to have a guy around for a change. Rider wasn't your typical male: he didn't play sports or chase girls or delight in causing physical pain to his buddies for laughs (although he wondered if he might like those things if his brain wasn't constantly bathed in estrogen), but he did enjoy bathroom humor, fantasized about fast cars, and would totally win a belching contest if given a chance. Living with Rachel, though, they spent most of their free time watching shows like *Pretty Little Liars* and reading paranormal teen romance novels.

"Sure," Rachel replied, trying to be nonchalant as she finagled open her locker door and placed her books inside with shaking fingers. She took a quick peek in her locker mirror to make sure no egregious facial defects had appeared since she left the house that morning and was fairly satisfied with her appearance, although she would definitely powder her nose and touch up her lipstick if Jason wasn't standing there staring. She patted her pocket to make sure her lunch money was still there, grateful she hadn't packed a lunch today. Jason didn't seem like the kind of guy who would bring a peanut butter sandwich in a paper bag.

Now that she thought about it, she wondered if Jason was wealthy. He did seem to have really nice clothes, and his perfectly straight teeth suggested he had worn braces at some point. Rachel's family wasn't poor by any means, but they weren't rich either. More like solidly middle class. Both her parents worked to be able to afford the nice home and newer cars they owned. Great — like she needed another reason to feel self-conscious around Jason. She decided she wasn't going to let herself worry about that. "Ready!" Rachel said, closing her locker and smiling at Jason.

The cafeteria was overflowing with rowdy teenagers

by the time they had purchased their chicken tenders and french fries, and Rachel wondered where Jason usually sat. She hadn't noticed him when she sat at the far end with the science club. He led the way in the opposite direction and approached a table filled with the kind of people she would never in a million years have tried to get to know.

The guys were big, muscular, and loud, probably athletes, and the girls were beautiful and haughty, their eyes permanently rolled back in their heads from looking disparagingly at everyone else. There were two seats open near the end of the table. Jason held out his hand, indicating that Rachel should choose first, so she took the last seat, the one farthest away from everyone else. Everyone turned to look as he introduced her.

"This is Rachel, she just moved here," he said with a wink and smile, and Rachel waved self-consciously. "This is Kelsey, Hannah, and Lindsey." He pointed towards the girls who dropped their looks of disdain just long enough to nod a welcome when he called each of their names. Rachel recognized Kelsey as the brunette Jason had schmoozed with during algebra the first day. A flick of his hand indicated Hanson, Kyle, and Zeke. The boys greeted her with a jumble of random noises that seemed to indicate approval and Jason beamed, seemingly pleased with their reactions.

"So tell me about yourself, Rachel," Jason purred as he settled in next to her, turning his back to the others. "I mean, I know you're from Michigan, and you like Batman movies and 80's music, but tell me about the real you."

A laugh, and a half-eaten french fry, escaped

Rachel's lips at that comment, and she blushed and grabbed a napkin to dab her mouth before replying. "I'm not sure those are my most definitive personality traits, but yeah, we just moved here for my dad's job, I do like most movies and music, although I generally prefer rom-coms to superheroes and Katy Perry to Debbie Gibson. I'm an only child, and I left my best friend, Paige, back in Michigan. What about you?" Rachel realized she didn't really know anything about the boy she was going to have her first date with, except that he was cute, good at opening lockers, and took the same math class as her.

Jason flicked his sandy blond waves and tossed a bite of food in his mouth, talking around the chicken tender. "Well, let's see, I've lived my whole life right here in Indy, which is why I'd like to see the rest of the world someday, I play several sports: football, basketball, soccer — but I'm not really that great at any of them, and I have an older brother who just left for college this year."

"See the world, huh? Are you planning to like, backpack through Europe after high school or something?" Rachel smirked, her mind playing into the assumption that his family was well-off.

"No, I think I want to be an airline pilot. Maybe fly internationally. Sounds exciting, doesn't it? Getting paid to travel all over the world." His eyes lit up with imagined adventures. "What are your plans for the future?"

"I really don't know yet," Rachel pondered. "I don't suppose there's such a thing as a professional TV watcher, is there? That's pretty much my greatest talent."

Soulmate

"Well, you could always model, if you're into that kind of thing." Jason said it casually, as if it was so obvious it could go without saying.

Rachel's eyes bugged out and she choked a little on her soda. Yeah, I'm a regular Tyra Banks! Rachel thought as she looked down at her ketchup-covered pile of fries and noticed a grease stain dotting the front of her blouse, presumably from the oil-soaked spuds. A glance at the other girls at the table revealed barely touched salads and bottles of sparkling water. Unlike Rachel, they had also clearly taken the time to touch up their makeup before lunch. "Um, yeah, I don't think I'm quite what they're looking for," she hedged, uncomfortably.

"What do you mean? You'd be perfect! That hair, those eyes, that... figure." His eyes roved up and down her body hungrily, stopping to linger at her breasts. Rachel flushed and put her hand up to her chest, wondering nervously if her shirt was exposing too much. Rider said nothing, but she could feel his revulsion at Jason's admiration. The girls across the table didn't seem surprised by Jason's lascivious appraisal, and Rachel wondered if they found his assessment accurate or were too uninterested in her to bother with a response. Their attention had turned to their cell phones which were being passed around between them as they compared pictures of favorite nail design ideas. She absent-mindedly hid her own short, stubby, unpainted nails by sitting on her hands.

"Dudes, party at my place this Saturday! You in, bros?" Hanson bellowed from the other end of the table. The already-rowdy boys took the news with excitement, celebrating with high fives, hoots, and chest-bumps, and even the girls abandoned their self-important prattling to offer smug smiles and murmurs of appreciation to Hanson. "Don't let me down by coming empty-handed, now, dudes. You gotta hook a brother up." Hanson smirked and fist-bumped Zeke who nodded emphatically and replied with a 'You know we got your back, dude!'

Jason turned back to Rachel with a grin and offered an invitation. "If I don't screw up our first date too badly, do you think you'd want to hang some more at Hanson's party?"

"Sounds great," Rachel replied, a thrill racing through her. She could hardly believe how readily the kids at this school were including her. Was it really her own exclusivity that had ostracized her from her peers back home? She hated to believe she had instigated her own rejection, but unless she had somehow developed stunning good looks and an incredibly fascinating personality in the last couple of weeks, clearly she was not as much of a loser as she had assumed herself to be.

Rider, silent but thoughtful, felt the weight of her former exclusion rest solidly on his shoulders. Of course she wasn't a loser like she had imagined. There was absolutely nothing wrong with her; it was him who had destroyed any chance of a normal life for her by demanding such a prominent role in it. He didn't understand how he had come to share her body with her, and they had never met or heard of anyone else who claimed a similar situation. As much as he loved the intimacy of their life together, he loved her even more, and he longed to free her from the bondage of his intrusion. While he did not know how to leave her, he promised himself he would strive to alleviate the stress of his relentless presence. He would stay quiet and passive, allowing her to focus on the outside world instead of his constant presence inside her head.

When the bell rang, Jason scooped up Rachel's tray along with his own and dropped them off at the receptacle. When his hands were free, he casually reached out to grab one of Rachel's. Stunned, Rachel looked down at their joined hands then back up to see an impish smile spreading across Jason's face. Her answering grin assured him she didn't mind the physical contact. As they walked slowly towards their classroom, she refrained from swinging their arms in happy abandon like she wanted to and instead concentrated on enjoying the feel of his large, masculine hand surrounding hers. In the back of her mind she wondered briefly what Rider thought of this development, but he was quiet, and instead of probing him for his opinion, her mind focused on the warm tingle radiating from their joined hands to the rest of her body.

The thrill continued as they entered their algebra class and spotted two adjacent seats in the back row. Rachel marveled at how quickly she had become the girl in the back of the room, cozying up to her boyfriend. The term shocked her as she thought it. Was Jason her boyfriend? Perhaps he would be, someday, but she thought it was a little too soon to consider him that. The idea excited her, though, and she spent most of the hour daydreaming about the possibility in between whispering to Jason when Mr. Volnar's back was turned.

When algebra ended, Jason walked with Rachel to

her art class, and his hand found hers again as they ambled slowly down the hall, giggling together about Mr. Volnar's strange set of idiosyncrasies. The distance between the two classrooms was substantial, but the walk was over way too soon, in Rachel's opinion.

As they reached the doorway, Rachel could sense the tension between them intensify, like watching a car zooming towards a cliff in an action movie. She could almost hear the background music escalate as her thoughts raced inevitably to the culmination of the scene. In a perfect movie-style ending, Jason turned to face her, and his hand reached up to stroke her cheek as his lips moved in for a kiss. They hovered, inches from her mouth, as his sparkling green eyes caught hers for a moment in silent request.

Overcome by his closeness and the frantic pulse racing through her body, she answered by slowly raising her lips to meet his in the softest wisp of a kiss. His mouth opened at her touch, and he pulled her close as his lips took hers, firm and demanding. His hold lasted just a moment, but that was all it took to claim her heart. He pulled away quickly and whispered a husky goodbye before turning away. Rachel's eyes followed him till he was lost in the crowd before turning to enter her own class in a lovesick daze.

She had just had her first kiss, by the cutest guy in the whole school, in front of everyone! Her cheeks burned at the thought, and she felt a moment of embarrassment, but the feeling was overcome by pleasure as she relived the salty taste of his lips on hers and the heat of his body as it closed the gap between them. Her skin tingled where his hands had grasped her, and her legs felt weak as she tried to walk. Her mind pulsed with the memory, blocking out all other sensations as she stumbled towards her desk.

Rider had never felt more alone than in that moment. His heart ached at the temporary isolation, and he longed to pull Rachel from her reverie and demand her attention. He could hear Jason's name pounding in her thoughts, and his own heart throbbed with envy. He felt a rush of hate flood through him, but it was overcome by a wave of love, and the two churned in his veins, creating a vortex of guilt and pain. He tried desperately to keep his thoughts hidden from Rachel as she slowly descended from her lofty exhilaration to a more maintainable level of giddy exuberance.

Rachel dropped into her chair with a goofy smile stretching her cheeks and slowly realized that people were staring at her: a few of the guys — who looked uncomfortably stimulated, a few of the girls — who looked a little jealous, a few others who looked disgusted, and Reggie, sitting right next to her, who grabbed his own hand and began kissing it exaggeratedly, rolling his eyes in passionate mockery. Rachel blushed and lowered her head in embarrassment. "Did I just make a total spectacle of myself, Reggie?" Rachel groaned.

"You def'nitly gave 'em somethin' to look at, dat's for sure!" His incredulous smile held a trace of censure. "You goin' out with him now or somethin'? It ain't none of my business, but that's kinda soon, isn't it?"

"Yeah, I guess, Reggie. I don't know, we just kind of hit it off, you know?" Rachel shrugged, unperturbed by his lack of confidence. She was still floating on a bubble of happiness and barely noticed his look of concern.

Reggie was the kind of guy who liked to keep it light and easy. He didn't get riled up by too many things, and he tried not to stick his nose in other people's business, but Rachel was new here, and she didn't know anything about Jason, or his reputation. He didn't know how to warn her, though, without hurting her feelings. He decided she probably wasn't ready to listen to any advice yet, anyway. He would just keep an eye on her and hope Jason showed his true colors before she got too involved with him. "Missed you at lunch today," he replied instead, "Tara too. Where she at, you know?"

"Oh, Tara had a dentist appointment, and Jason asked me to sit with him and meet some of his friends. What did you guys talk about?" she asked, more out of politeness than actual interest. She was pretty sure she wouldn't understand it anyway.

Her question distracted him for a moment as he recalled the intense discussion they'd had about the odds of a solar flare devastating the global technological infrastructure, but the thought of Rachel hanging out with Jason's low-life group of friends usurped his concern about a world-wide power failure and he decided to offer some advice after all. "Them peeps that he likes to hang with, they be like, bad news, you know what I'm sayin'?" Reggie offered in the gentlest way possible. He definitely did not like criticizing other people, but he was worried about Rachel.

"They looked kind of stuck up when I first saw them, but they were nice to me," Rachel replied, a little defensively, thoughts of her own past rejection still fresh in her mind. "They even invited me to a party on Saturday."

"They just ain't known for being nice, if you know what I mean," Reggie explained. Before they had a chance to discuss it further, the assistant began passing out supplies for their next project and Rachel's attention was diverted to the teacher's explanation of surrealism. Surreal — that's exactly how this whole thing feels right now! Rachel thought to herself. I can't believe I just kissed a boy in front of the entire class then defended the integrity of the homecoming court to my friend the science geek! How bizarre has my life become? Rider agreed wholeheartedly. Her new world was certainly causing a change in his.

Chapter Eleven

Despite her concern over Rider's recent silence, Rachel could not contain the smile that lit up her face on Thursday as she boarded the bus for school. "Okay, flashlight face, what is up with you?" Tara asked in her typical sarcastic tone as Rachel plopped onto the bench next to her. Figuring that, after kissing Jason in front of the whole class, her secret was pretty much out, Rachel decided there was no point in trying to keep quiet about it.

"I'm just excited about my date tomorrow." Rachel tried to reply nonchalantly, but her giddiness was too overwhelming, so she quickly dropped the act and spilled all the juicy details to Tara. "It's my first date, and I'm technically not even allowed to date yet, so please don't say anything to my parents, but we're going to be surrounded by other people, so it's not like my virtue is at risk or anything! And it's with THE CUTEST GUY in the whole school, IMHO," Rachel squealed with excitement.

"Wow, Rachel, that's amazing! You've been here

like four days and you already got asked out? I've lived here for 15 years, and the closest I've ever gotten to a date was when the rest of the club bailed and Garrett and I ended up watching the last space shuttle launch together at his house, with his little sisters," Tara complained. "So who's the lucky guy?"

"Jason Decatur. Do you know him? What am I saying? You have to know him; he's like a supermodel! Wait, is there such a thing as a guy supermodel? I don't know, but he could definitely be one!" Rachel rambled, oblivious to Tara's apprehensive silence.

"Oh wow," Tara managed to reply, with just a little hesitation. She wanted to warn her of Jason's Don Juan reputation, but she hated to burst her new friend's bubble. "So where are you two going?"

"He's meeting me at the concert in the park tomorrow night — some retro 80's band. Hey, you guys should go! I told my mom I was meeting some friends there, so if you went, I wouldn't even be lying!" Rachel giggled.

"Yeah, that sound's cool. Maybe I will," Tara replied. "So how'd you meet Jason?"

"He helped me get my locker open on my first day, and then I saw him again at the movie theater, plus he's in my algebra class. It's, like, fate or something; we just keep bumping into each other! He invited me to sit with him at lunch yesterday and after Algebra, he kissed me in the hallway! It was so totally amazing! My first kiss, in front of everyone! I wonder if it was his first kiss, too..."

"Unfortunately, it's not. He's actually had quite a few girlfriends already," Tara replied sourly, the thought of Jason's lechery turning her stomach. "I think Jason is more interested in getting in your pants than winning your heart."

"Wow, Tara, that's... really harsh. Thanks for the compliment," Rachel snarled, disgusted by her friend's appraisal. How could she possibly know anything about Jason's feelings for her? The old, ugly pain of rejection stabbed like a knife ripping open a barely-closed wound. "I'm glad to know you think I could never attract a cute guy unless he has an ulterior motive!" The bus pulled to a stop in front of the school and Rachel hurried off, glad to escape the conversation. She couldn't believe how mean Tara had been! And here she thought Tara might actually become a good friend. Now she dreaded the thought of even seeing her in literature class.

"Hi, Beautiful," a sexy voice crooned in her ear as she angrily stuffed her backpack into her locker. The ice around her heart immediately started to melt at the sound of his voice, and she turned to see Jason's dazzling eyes staring straight into her soul.

"Hi," she stuttered, her face warming with pleasure as he stared at her like a man seeing the sunrise for the first time.

"How are you today?" He asked sincerely, not with the fleeting interest of common courtesy, but with genuine concern etched across his features.

"Better now." Rachel smiled in response. "You

look happy."

"Why wouldn't I be? I have an incredible weekend planned with my amazing new girlfriend," Jason declared, throwing his arm around Rachel's shoulders and pulling her close for a kiss. Flames of desire engulfed her as she let herself relax into his embrace, and her irritation disintegrated into ash. "May I escort you to your first class?" Jason offered chivalrously, turning them towards the door to her chemistry class.

"I'm pretty sure I can find it on my own," Rachel smirked, but her hand reached up to grasp his and she happily let him lead her to her desk.

"I'll meet you at your locker before lunch," Jason promised and kissed her on the nose before sauntering out of the classroom. At the door, he turned and winked before disappearing into the hall.

Rachel felt someone's gaze directed at her and turned to see Kelsey, Jason's leggy friend, staring at her. Rachel offered her a small smile and got a nod in return. Definitely better than a scowl. I guess I passed her coolness test, Rachel thought sarcastically.

Her mind wandered the rest of first period, contrasting her friends' warnings about Jason with his seemingly genuine attraction to her. Sure, he'd kissed her and complimented her appearance, but it didn't seem lewd or lascivious, just flattering and romantic. Didn't all guys do that with their girlfriends? Maybe he had gone out with a lot of girls, but that was no surprise, as gorgeous as he was. Surely he could have any girl he wanted. They were probably throwing themselves at him left and right! He wasn't paying attention to any other girls, though. He only had eyes for Rachel.

She couldn't figure out why, when no one else had ever thought she was special, but here, people saw her differently than before. Here she wasn't a freak with an imaginary friend and a reputation for being off her rocker. Here she was somebody worth knowing and apparently beautiful, at least in Jason's eyes.

Tara just didn't really know Jason, Rachel decided. All she knew was that he'd had other girlfriends in the past. She was probably a little jealous, too. Who wouldn't be? She admitted she'd never had a date before. She probably had an unrequited crush on Jason. Tara wasn't exactly attractive. Sure, once you got to know her she was cool, but she wasn't very pretty, and she hung out with a bunch of nerds, so how could she possibly expect to attract the cutest boy in the whole school?

Rachel didn't want to ask Rider his opinion; she already knew he didn't like Jason, or even the idea of another guy in her life, but she longed to talk to him about it. Rider had always been her biggest confidante; she shared everything with him. His silence was deafening.

"I'm happy for you," Rider offered, sensing her hesitation. "I was wrong to try to keep you to myself. You have every right to have a boyfriend if you want, and I'll try not to hate him, even if I do think he's a total douche bag," Rider joked. He knew his reticence towards the relationship was unfair, if not unwarranted. "Just don't forget about me completely, okay?" He pleaded, his light-hearted tone belying his true fear.

"Thank you, Rider, that means a lot," Rachel thought, immensely relieved to reach some reconciliation with her best friend. "And how could I ever forget you, huh? You never shut up!" she teased. But that wasn't the truth. Rider had shown her just how capable he was of staying silent, and she hadn't liked it at all.

* * * * * * *

Rachel approached her 3rd period classroom with trepidation, unsure how her encounter with Tara should be resolved. She didn't have to consider it too long, though, as Tara rushed to her side the moment she saw Rachel enter the room.

"I'm so sorry for what I said on the bus, Rachel," Tara apologized, a look of anguish on her face. "I didn't mean it like that at all. You're beautiful and smart and any guy would be lucky to go out with you! I'm just not sure Jason really appreciates that, you know?"

The apology quickly melted the ice in Rachel's heart. "It's okay, Tara, I forgive you. I know you didn't mean to hurt me. But Jason really cares about me. You should give him a chance. I know he seems way too cool, but he's just like everybody else, only, well, hotter, I guess!" Rachel felt her heart lift as the strings of tension between them were cut. Life was so much more pleasant when you weren't at odds with all your friends.

"Maybe so, but just be careful, okay? I don't want

to see you get hurt by some guy," Tara conceded.

"Don't worry, I can take care of myself. Now you, on the other hand, could definitely use some help in the guy department. It's totally obvious you have a thing for Tyler, so what are you doing about it?" Rachel goaded, grateful they had managed to make up but still anxious to take the spotlight off her relationship with Jason.

"I've liked him forever, but he sees me as just another one of the guys, I think." Tara's eyes dropped depreciatively down her boyish figure.

"I don't know, maybe he's just shy. Maybe you should ask him out if he's not smart enough to ask you."

"But what if he doesn't like me that way? It would totally ruin the group dynamic. And why would he like me? He's superior to me in every way: looks, intelligence, even charisma." Tara counted off Tyler's winning traits on her fingers.

"Oh, Tara, you're a piece of work, you know that?" Rachel rolled her eyes. "That's exactly why Tyler would like you! You're funny, and you talk like a science professor, which I think he totally digs, and you're a really good friend, too." Rachel offered a smile of appreciation. "Look, why don't you let me help you? We could go to the concert together, like a double date! You ask Tyler if he wants to go and I'll help you do your hair and makeup. My mom can take us both to the park, and you can meet up with Tyler while I hang out with Jason." She started to get excited at the prospect of giving Tara a makeover.

"I don't know if I'm brave enough to ask him on a date, Rachel." Tara's hand absent-mindedly smoothed her lank hair.

Rachel's eyes grew wide as an idea came to her, and she grinned mischievously. "You know what, maybe you don't even have to. I'll suggest it to him in gym class today. I can feel him out for you, see if there's any interest. Maybe if I put the idea in his head, he'll be brave enough to ask you!"

Tara looked skeptical, but she half-heartedly agreed to the plan, and the two spent the rest of the period day-dreaming about the upcoming weekend. When the bell rang, Rachel jumped up and headed for the door in a rush, excited to see Jason again.

"Hey, aren't you eating lunch with us?" Tara asked.

"No, Jason said he'd meet me at my locker," Rachel explained with a grin and hurried off to find her starry-eyed dream guy, while Tara wondered if someday soon she would be happily running off to meet her own boyfriend. She was doubtful but anxious to see what would happen. Was a little nudge all it would take for Tyler to ask her out, like Rachel presumed? She just prayed that Rachel would be subtle about it. How awkward would it be if Tyler wasn't interested but he knew Tara was? She pondered these dilemmas while making her way to her usual table in the lunch room.

The rest of the gang was already there, and her usual spot across from Tyler was glaringly empty. It felt uncomfortable just knowing that she had considered the possibility of going out with him. Would he see it in her face when she looked at him? She understood calculus and had researched nanotechnology; she had a pretty good grasp on the basics of quantum mechanics. But boys? They were a mystery to her, and attracting them seemed like an elusive science, one they didn't teach in AP Chemistry or even Human Physiology. How did other girls figure this out? Was it really just a pretty face and a nice figure that got a boy's attention? Surely not, she decided as she glanced at Eve, who was really quite attractive but still socially challenged.

"Where's Rachel?" Eve questioned, catching Tara's glance.

"She's sitting with Jason Decatur, her new boyfriend," Tara answered warily. Eve raised a brow in surprise. "I know, I tried to warn her, but she seems convinced that he's her Romeo," Tara said with a roll of her eyes. Eve wasn't one to gossip, so she didn't ask for any details, and Tara was quickly distracted by talk of a movie marathon that Reggie was hosting that Saturday. Maybe she would invite Rachel, she considered. Anything to distract her from Jason Decatur.

* * * * * * *

Rachel floated into her art class on a cloud of romantic delirium. Jason had bought her lunch and regaled her with his dreams of travel to exotic locations and to her delight, he included her in his fantasies of world-wide adventure. He imagined them spending a luxurious holiday in a Parisian mansion, cavorting through the streets of London, frolicking on a tropical island in the Caribbean, and dining at a famous restaurant in the heart of Milan.

She could easily picture herself in his dreams, her plate of cafeteria spaghetti becoming a gourmet Italian meal as they toasted their future with pints of milk in lieu of sparkling champagne.

After lunch, Jason had proudly held her hand to and from class and kissed her passionately in front of the art room again, and Rachel was dreaming of time alone with him the following night. She longed to run her hands down his muscular torso and kiss a path from his lips to his chest. She had never been this physically intimate with a boy before, and it set afire parts of her that had lain dormant until now.

"Girl, you gonn' set off the smoke alarm, you keep smooching like that!" Reggie teased as Rachel took her seat next to him in a lovesick fog. She blushed as she imagined the spectacle they had created.

"Have you ever been in love, Reggie? It's amazing…" Rachel said dreamily, her eyes unfocused as she pictured herself strolling with Jason on the banks of the Seine.

"I don't know 'bout that kinda lovin', but I got some pretty passionate feelin's 'bout chicken wings. So I think I know how you feel, gurl," Reggie teased, an easy smile on his face. It was hard not to like Reggie.

Rachel started to laugh, and, already riding an emotional high, lost control and tumbled into a fit of giggles. Her classmates, many who were still staring after her dramatic lip lock, began to gawk overtly at her outburst. Rachel barely managed to quiet her chuckling before the

Kellie McAllen

teacher came in, but she heard little of the directions as she rode the wave of her euphoria.

"Hey Rachel," Reggie whispered once the teacher had finished explaining the project and prompted the students to start, "if you like to laugh like a crazy person, why doncha come over to my place on Saturday. We're watchin' *Revenge of the Nerds,* and I think you might like it."

"Oh, that sounds fun, Reg, but I'm going to a party with Jason Saturday night."

"That's all right, we gun' start 'bout noon, cuz there like four movies, so you could catch one or two of 'em, if you want. Tara 'n Eve'll be there."

"Oooh, oooh, I wanna watch 'em!" Rider interjected excitedly. "I like making fun of nerds!"

"You shouldn't, because you ARE a nerd, Rider!" Rachel retorted.

"Yeah, maybe I will." Rachel decided, giving Reggie a big grin. She was hoping to avoid doing chores this weekend, and her mom, who still felt guilty about the move, would probably give her a pass if she had a chance to hang out with some friends. "Should I bring something?" she asked, remembering Hanson's admonition not to come to his party empty-handed.

"I'm gonna serve some of my famous chicken wings." Reggie's chest puffed with pride. "Tyler'll bring some chips, and Tara makes some brownies dat be outta this world, so it's all covered, 'less you wanna bring some drinks or somethin'. Garrett drinks the Dew by the gallon," Reggie explained, shaking his head as he remembered how crazy Garrett got the last time he had access to a large supply of Mountain Dew. Rachel nodded. It would be easy enough to raid the fridge for some 2-liters of soda. Her dad was a pretty big fan of the Dew, too.

Reggie wrote down his phone number and address for Rachel and the two got to work on their art projects. They were supposed to create surrealistic drawings, and Rachel decided there could be nothing more surreal than a guy as amazing as Jason kissing her in front of everybody.

* * * * * * *

Rachel hated gym class normally, all that running and sweating and pointless ball-chasing. But today she was excited when it was finally time to suit up for P.E. She had never played matchmaker before, but she was thrilled at the idea of setting up Tara and Tyler. They were perfect for each other, anyone could see that, and all it should take was a little persuasion to motivate Tyler to act. She contemplated her approach as she changed into her navy blue gym shorts and gray Indy High tee, keeping her nose plugged against the dirty sock smell of the locker room. She hoped she would get a chance to talk to him. They had just finished a unit on volleyball, and she wasn't sure what torture Mr. Klein had in store for them today.

"Okay, you spoiled rotten little maggots, get out here and stretch out!" Coach Klein hollered blindly into the locker room. Mr. Klein was under the impression that derogatory commands were the best motivation for high school students. Noticing the way most of the kids blithely ignored him, Rachel decided he must not know much about teenagers.

"Now that most of you finally know how to hit a ball over a net, it's time to build up your endurance so you can make it through an entire game without passing out like a bunch of pansies!" Coach Klein's face was red with exertion, and his whistle bounced against his chest every time he smacked his clipboard against his hand. "So today, you're gonna run till you wanna pass out, and then you're gonna run a little longer!" The announcement was met with a chorus of groans, and the students ambled as slowly as possible out to the track.

As much as she hated running, Rachel was pleased with today's activity because it meant she would have a chance to talk to Tyler, assuming she could keep up with him. Figuring she better catch him while she still had the energy to actually run, Rachel sprinted to the front of the group where Tyler was and matched her pace to his.

"Hi Tyler!" she greeted him, trying hard not to sound out of breath already.

"Hey, Rachel." Tyler's voice was cheerful. "Missed you at lunch the last couple days."

"Yeah, I was sitting with... some other people I met." Rachel wasn't sure if she should mention Jason's name or not. Tyler didn't seem to have a very high opinion of him, and she didn't want that to deter him from joining them on Friday.

"Tara said you're going out with Jason Decatur." So much for being vague.

"Well, he asked me to go to this concert with him tomorrow night in the park," Rachel explained, still trying to downplay the rapid development of their relationship. This conversation was supposed to be about Tara, not Jason.

"Oh yeah, that 80's tribute band, Pistols n' Lilies; I've heard they're pretty good. I was thinking about going to that concert."

"You should!" Rachel practically shouted. Tyler was making this so easy. "I mean, you would probably really like it," she added, lowering her voice a few octaves. "Maybe we could double date! Wouldn't that be fun?"

Rachel could almost see the gears turning in Tyler's head as his expression shifted from excitement, to regret, to hopefulness, and back down to disappointment. "That sounds great except for one minor problem, Rachel. I don't have a date," Tyler admitted quietly, hanging his head.

"Well, we'll just have to find you one, then!" Rachel gave a suggestive grin.

"Good luck with that." Tyler dropped his head, staring at his tennis shoes. "None of the girls in this school have ever even noticed me." *My only hope was that some hot new girl would show up and fall for me, but look how that turned out — the most popular guy in the school got to her first!* Tyler thought but didn't dare speak out loud.

"That is definitely not true, Tyler!" Rachel said breathlessly. She was way too out of shape to run and talk at the same time. Fortunately, Tyler didn't seem to be faring much better. Unable to go any farther, she came to a halt and bent at the waist to catch her breath for a moment before attempting the denouement.

When she lifted her head, Tyler was breathing loudly and rapidly with his hands on his hips, staring, waiting for an explanation. Oops! Rachel thought. Maybe I said too much. She didn't want to reveal Tara's feelings until she was sure they were reciprocated.

"You are a really great guy, Tyler," Rachel backpedaled, "and I'm sure there are lots of girls who would go out with you if you just asked them. When was the last time you asked a girl out, anyway?"

"Uh, let me think… never," Tyler confessed.

"Tyler! You can't expect to get a date if you never ask anyone out! I know this is the 21st century and there's women's lib and all that, but girls still expect the boy to do the asking. That's just the way it is."

A whistle screeched somewhere behind them, and they turned to see Coach pointing at them with daggers for eyes. He motioned for them to keep moving, so they began to jog again, hardly faster than a walk. Most of the other students were slowing down too, so hopefully Coach wouldn't notice them as long as they weren't standing still.

"What kind of girl are you interested in, anyway?" Rachel asked, hoping to steer the conversation towards

Tara.

"I guess someone who likes the same things I do, someone I can be myself around," Tyler responded thoughtfully.

"Interpretation: a geek with boobs," Rider offered, and Rachel choked on a laugh.

"Anybody in particular?" Rachel hinted, ignoring Rider, trying to get Tyler to mention Tara's name. She had a pretty good idea that he liked her, but she wanted him to say it. What she didn't know was that Tyler was afraid to bring up Tara too, for fear that Rachel might tell her.

"Maybe..." Tyler hedged.

Out of patience, Rachel decided to go for broke. "Tyler, I think you should ask Tara. Don't you think you two would be great together?" Rachel watched closely for his reaction, but he quickly lowered his head.

"Tara is... really special," Tyler acknowledged. "We've been friends for a long time. What if she's not interested? I don't want to ruin things with her."

"Tyler." Rachel stopped and turned to face him, sure now that it was safe to share Tara's secret. "Tara said almost the exact same thing to me this morning — when she was talking about you."

Tyler's blush grew to a flush of excitement as realization dawned, and he stared in awe at Rachel. "Tara likes me?" he questioned, still in shock that he could have completely missed her interest.

"Yes, you doofus! She's had a crush on you forever! I noticed it the first day I got here. That's why I didn't want to encourage you when you flirted with me. I knew she wanted you!"

"I didn't flirt with you; only girls flirt," Tyler defended himself. "You really could tell right away that she liked me?"

"Guys flirt too, and you definitely flirted with me, but that's not the point! Of course I could tell right away that she liked you, she was staring at you like a homeless beggar at the all-you-can-eat buffet!"

"Mmmm, speaking of buffets, when was the last time you took me to one, huh? You know how I feel about that never-ending dessert bar…," Rider quipped.

"Shut up, Rider, I'm trying to have a serious conversation here!"

"Wow, I did not see that. You really think she'd say yes if I asked her out?" Tyler asked in a little-boy voice, squeaky with insecurity.

"Yes, Tyler, 100% certain. But you've got to do it today cuz the concert's tomorrow," Rachel demanded, sure that he would lose his nerve if he waited.

"Well, I don't normally see her after last period. I could call her tonight, though."

"No, absolutely not. You have to ask her face to

face. Stop by her locker as soon as class is over. I'll be waiting to hear all about it on the bus ride home!"

Mercifully, Coach Klein blew his whistle to call the students back in, and Rachel and Tyler gratefully walked back to the gym. "Don't wuss out on me now, Tyler!" Rachel called as Tyler headed for the boy's locker room. A nervous smile played across his lips as he dunked his head and turned his back on her.

Maybe I ought to follow him, Rachel thought as she wiped the sweat from her brow with the bottom of her tee shirt. He'd probably notice her lurking and get freaked out, though. She'd just have to trust that she'd done a good enough job convincing him of Tara's interest. Pretty good for your first time! She thought, thrilled with how smoothly the whole thing had gone. Now she just had to wait a few minutes to hear all about it from Tara.

* * * * * * *

Rachel could tell right away by the huge smile on Tara's face that Tyler had done it. She practically floated up the steps and into the seat next to Rachel.

"Tell me all about it!" Rachel demanded, turning in her seat to face Tara. She wanted to see the fruits of her labor in the blissed out expression on Tara's face, and she wanted to hear all the juicy details since she hadn't been there to witness it.

"He managed to croak out a request for a date, she got doe-eyed and said yes, and they both tripped on their untied shoe laces in their hurry to get away from each other. End of story!" Rider mocked. "Do we really need to hear all the gory details?" Rider was not a big fan of girl talk.

"Shush! Yes we do! Now be quiet so I can enjoy this!"

"So Tyler stopped by my locker after school and was acting kind of weird," Tara hinted, a devilish smile on her lips. "He asked me if I liked 80's music."

"And...," Rachel encouraged, nodding.

"And I told him I loved it, of course! I almost mentioned the concert myself, but I wanted to let him since it looked like he was going to." Tara's plain face lit up with excitement, increasing her attractiveness tenfold.

Rachel's smile widened and her head started to bob excitedly. "Go on...!"

"So he did it! He asked me if I wanted to go with him to see it, and I said yes, and we both were so freaked out our sympathetic nervous systems went into hyperdrive and we blushed and stuttered and essentially turned into gibbering morons! I told him to meet me there since I figured you and I were riding together; that is, if you're still willing to do my hair?" Tara probed hesitantly.

"Absolutely. Why don't you come home with me tomorrow afternoon? I'll make you look gorgeous. Tyler won't even be able to hear the music he'll be so awestruck by how fabulous you are!" Rachel giggled eagerly.

"What should I wear?" Tara put a finger to her lip as she contemplated. "I could raid my mom's old clothes for some neon and spandex, I suppose…"

Rachel's eyes bugged out and she grabbed Tara's shoulders. "No, no, no. Definitely not! Don't worry about it; I'll loan you something of mine," Rachel offered, worried about what wardrobe atrocity Tara might commit if she tried to dress herself for the occasion.

"Fabulous, it's all planned out. Can we please talk about something else now?" Rider whined, "All this girl talk is making my ears bleed!"

As if on cue, Tara changed the subject to Reggie's upcoming movie marathon and was thrilled to hear that he had already invited Rachel and she was planning to go. The two chatted till their bus reached Rachel's block, and the girls impulsively hugged before saying goodbye.

"Okay, I'm proud of you. You did your good deed for the day. But all this estrogen is gagging me. Can we watch some wrestling or something now?" Rider snarked. Rachel just grinned. She did feel pretty darn good about herself. Rider was secretly proud of her, too. He thought it was really sweet of her to help out her friends like that.

"Oh, but I was hoping you'd help me pick out my outfit for tomorrow!" she teased, and headed straight for her closet. She had two outfits to design!

Chapter Twelve

"No way. I draw the line at heels. My sense of co-ordination is just not developed enough to keep from embarrassing myself in front of Tyler while wearing those boots. My Converse will just have to do." Tara pulled nervously on the hem of the forest green sweater dress that ended mid-thigh. She was definitely not used to showing this much leg, even if it was covered with sheer black leggings.

Rachel decided Tara looked good enough without the boots and didn't press the issue. She had added soft curls to Tara's normally unstyled hair and played up her eyes with liner, mascara, and a sweep of bronze eye shadow. Her lips were coated in a totally kissable plum-tinted balm, and her dress was cinched in at the waist with a wide leather belt that emphasized the feminine shape Tara normally hid under loose tee shirts. The black Converse sneakers were not great, but they were a little more practical that the high-heeled boots Rachel had offered.

"Well, you look great, so you don't have anything to worry about," Rachel reassured her, checking her own reflection one last time before grabbing her purse and heading for the stairs. Focusing on Tara had distracted her from her own first date jitters, but now that it was time to leave she could feel her stomach clenching up into a tight ball of nerves.

"Don't you girls look lovely!" Mrs. Masterson exclaimed as Tara and Rachel entered the kitchen. Rachel hoped they didn't look too lovely, or her parents might suspect this was more than just a girls' night. Apparently their appearance didn't raise any red flags because Mary grabbed her keys off the counter with a smile and headed for the door. The drive to the park was nerve-wracking for Rachel, but Tara blithely made small talk with Mrs. Masterson so Rachel could concentrate fully on being nervous.

"I'll pick you up right here at 9," Mary said as she pulled into the parking lot and idled in front of the park entrance. "Will you need a ride home, Tara?"

"No ma'am, my mom will come for me. Thanks so much for taking me, though!" Tara chirped brightly.

"You're welcome, sweetie. I'm glad to see Rachel has made such a nice friend. I hope you girls have fun. What kind of concert is this, anyway?"

"It's an 80's retro band. They do mostly really old songs, but they're pretty cool," Tara answered, and Rachel grimaced.

"I love 80's music!" Mary squealed and Tara's eyes

widened in alarm. "Rachel, why didn't you tell me that earlier? I could have come with you! You know how much I like classic rock, but I already agreed to go to Debbie Johnson's Mary Kay party," Mary explained with a frown. Tara and Rachel both sighed in relief.

"Sorry, Mom. I didn't think. Maybe next time, okay?" Rachel offered, climbing quickly from the car.

"That could've been disastrous." Tara apologized as the two waved goodbye to Rachel's mother.

"Yeah, less is always more when it comes to my mother. Usually, the more I tell her, the more likely she is to freak out," Rachel explained.

"My mother is just the opposite; she wants to know every detail or she gets suspicious," Tara began, but then her eyes glazed over as she stared over Rachel's shoulder into the crowd.

Rachel turned around to see Tyler heading towards them, a huge smile on his face. He had made an attempt to dress for the occasion with a polo shirt instead of his usual tee and khakis instead of jeans. Both had the slightly rumpled look of clothes that have been squished into the back of the closet for a long time, but at least he had tried. He didn't have his own personal fashion assistant for the night like Tara had. As he approached, he gave a quick glance towards Rachel and nodded hello, but then his eyes returned to Tara like laser beams cutting a path straight to her figure.

"Hi Rachel." Tyler gave another glance her way

then turned straight back to Tara. "Tara, you look amazing!"

Tara blushed and lowered her gaze to the ground as Tyler's eyes took in every inch of her. "Thanks, Ty, you look good, too."

"I'm gonna go look for Jason, okay? You two have fun together!" Rachel gave a quick wave and headed off into the crowd. It was a surprisingly eclectic mix of people — mostly middle-aged couples, of course, out on a date night with their spouses, their 80's style outfits clearly original. But there were also quite a few young people, teens and twenty-somethings — a testament to the popularity of tonight's performers.

It got a little easier to see as Rachel approached the bandstand because most of the audience had settled onto blankets and lawn chairs. Jason had promised to save them a spot near the front, so Rachel scanned the space near the stage for a sandy-haired hottie sitting alone. She almost missed him, her eyes passing over the group of teens standing together, laughing and talking, but then he turned his head and caught sight of her scanning the crowd. His face lit up in recognition and he waved, flashing his perfect white smile. Rachel felt a touch of irritation that he was not alone, but it quickly faded as his attention immediately shifted towards her and he made his way through the audience to her side.

"Hi gorgeous, you look great." His eyes roamed up and down her body, appraising, and he kissed her deeply, his arms wrapping around her body to pull her close and his hands caressing her back. The heat of his touch blazed through her sweater and sent a flame of fire racing through her whole body. She returned his embrace, her hands outlining the taut muscles of his back as she leaned into the kiss, oblivious to the crowd of onlookers witnessing their display. The spell was broken by the sound of a guitar, pealing off an opening riff to welcome the band to the stage. Jason's lips pulled away slowly as he reached for her hand to lead her to their blanket.

The crowd jumped to their feet, making passage more difficult as the band climbed onto the stage and erupted into a very authentic version of "Welcome to the Jungle." Rachel felt her nerves give way to excitement, and she and Jason quickly joined in the revelry, clapping and singing loudly as the lead singer whipped his hair and gyrated his hips spasmodically.

Welcome to the jungle

It gets worse here every day

Ya learn to live like an animal

In the jungle where we play

If you got a hunger for what you see

You'll take it eventually

You can have anything you want

But you better not take it from me

Rachel sang along as well as she could, but Jason seemed to know most of the words and his voice was surprisingly smooth as he belted out the lyrics enthusiastically.

His eyes caught Rachel's on some of the lines, and she felt like he was singing the words just for her. The band segued into Quiet Riot's "Come on Feel the Noise", and Rachel had an easier time keeping up with the simple chorus as they pumped their fists in exultation and declared their intention to get wild, wild, wild. Rachel's euphoria left her panting and breathless, and she giggled as her voice cracked and wavered.

Jason handed her a soda bottle when he heard her voice getting raspy, and she gratefully took a large gulp and then another. The taste seemed different somehow, and it burned a little as it slid down her throat, but Rachel just chalked it up to her dehydration. She took a few more deep swallows before handing it back to Jason. He was dancing unreservedly and she felt her own inhibitions crumbling as she jumped wildly up and down in time to the music. The band switched to Def Leppard, and Rachel began to feel hot, sticky, sweet as Jason crooned in her ear to pour some sugar on him. The band encouraged him to squeeze a little, squeeze a little, tease a little more, and he grabbed her close from behind and began to grind his hips against her as his hands roamed across her body.

Rachel felt her bones liquefy as Jason's hands touched every inch of her. She leaned against him and closed her eyes to concentrate on the feeling of his body against hers as the music finally slowed into a ballad. The rest of the crowd began to settle into their chairs as the band serenaded them with a love song, and Jason pulled Rachel down to the blanket and began to kiss her gently, his hand caressing her cheek then slowly sliding down her neck to her chest.

"Is this love that I'm feeling? Is this the love that I've been searching for?" Jason purred the lyrics to the song as he trailed kisses down her throat. Rachel's heart thrummed with passion as the words registered in her mind. Was Jason saying he was in love with her? She wasn't sure exactly what she felt for him, but she knew she'd never felt so strongly about anything before. She returned his kisses, pulling his lips back to hers in a deep embrace as the song ended. Rider had been enjoying the concert but was about to throw a conniption at the intense fondling when the sound of clapping interrupted their revelry. The band broke for intermission and the crowd began to stir as the audience got up to mingle with friends or grab a bite from the concession stands.

"Are you hungry?" Jason asked, the spell of their passion broken by the distraction. He reached into the cooler and pulled out another bottle of soda and some snacks. Rachel gratefully accepted the soda and nibbled eagerly on a sandwich. "Do you like the band?" he asked, taking a sip and leaning back on his hand with a look of satisfaction.

"They're awesome!" Rachel gave a wide smile, tossing her sweat-dampened hair behind her shoulder. "This is amazing. We never had anything this cool to do back in Michigan, at least not in my hometown. Do they have these concerts often?"

"Yeah, they have different bands each time, but this one is my favorite. My dad listens to this kind of music around the house all the time, so I guess that's why I'm so into it," Jason explained.

"I've heard a lot of these songs before, but never live like this. The atmosphere here is like, intoxicating!" Her voice sounded loud in her own head.

Jason chuckled. "Well, that might be the alcohol you've been guzzling."

"What?!" Rachel sputtered, and her eyes widened in shock as she looked down at the bottle in her hand. "I thought this was soda!"

"It is, sort of. Only I poured some out and filled it back up with rum. Nobody can tell that way. Haven't you ever had rum and coke?"

"Oh, yeah, sure," Rachel lied impulsively. She didn't want to look naïve in front of Jason. He was already way cooler than her as it was.

Rachel saw Tara and Tyler approaching just then, and she eagerly waved at them, putting the cap back on the soda bottle and tucking it out of sight. Tara had a grin on her face, so Rachel was pretty sure her date was going okay. They chatted for a few minutes about the music and the other people who were there until the band took the stage again, and Tara and Tyler headed back to their seats.

"Are you friends with them?" Jason asked incredulously after they had left.

"Yeah, I met Tara on the bus my first day. She was really nice to me. She introduced me to Tyler, but this is actually their first date. I sort of hooked them up," Rachel admitted sheepishly.

"They don't really seem like your type, if you know what I mean," Jason insinuated.

"They're in the science club and they're kind of geeky, but they're really great people once you get to know them," Rachel responded, a little bothered by Jason's attitude.

"Of course, I didn't mean anything," Jason backpedaled, sensing Rachel's irritation. "If you like them, I'm sure I would too." He smiled, brushing a hand against her cheek. Rachel warmed to his touch and smiled softly.

"He's such a faker, Rachel. Can't you see that?" Rider complained. "He thinks Tara and Tyler are losers, and he thinks you're strange for being friends with them."

"He just doesn't know them yet, Rider. Can't you see that he's trying?"

"He's trying to get into your pants, that what I see."

"Well, it's working. I just might let him. No one has ever treated me as special as Jason does!"

"Rachel, no!" Rider thought so loudly that Rachel was almost sure that Jason could hear him. "Just because he makes you feel good doesn't mean he's good for you! He's already got you drinking and making out in front of the whole world!"

"Rachel, are you okay?" Jason asked, looking at her strangely. "You look a little spaced out."

Rachel's eyes snapped back into focus, and her attention returned to the world around her. She gave Jason a big smile. "Sorry. Just daydreaming, I guess!"

"Well, I hope I was in your dreams," Jason cooed as he leaned in for another kiss, this time placing his hand precariously close to her breast. Rachel purposely leaned into his touch. The band was playing slower music now, and Rachel felt like they could see into her soul as they sang about sweet surrender. She gave herself over to the feeling and let Jason caress her till her body melted into his.

"I know a place we can go, if you want to be alone," Jason whispered, teasing her neck with kisses.

Rachel's eyes popped open, and she struggled to form a response. She wasn't even sure how she really felt. "I don't... I mean, my mom is picking me up in a little bit, so... I better not leave."

"I can take you home instead. Why don't you just call her? Save her a trip. She'd probably appreciate it," Jason suggested smoothly, his hand doing distracting things to her body.

Rachel was loathe to admit she wasn't technically supposed to even be with a boy since she wasn't allowed to date yet. "She gets kind of paranoid about me riding with people she doesn't know," Rachel hedged.

"Hmm, well I guess you better introduce us then, so she won't be so nervous next time." Jason's fingers trailed along her collarbone, sending electric pulses through her brain.

That was definitely out of the question. "Maybe next time," Rachel answered quickly. "She... she's... a little cranky today." That sounded really lame, but Rachel couldn't think of a better excuse.

Jason looked a little incredulous, but he just smiled and nodded. "Beware of cranky mothers. Got it. Maybe some other time."

Rider breathed a sigh of relief that Rachel had managed to avert Jason's romantic intentions. He was definitely not prepared to watch her go all the way with Lover Boy tonight.

The band was starting to speed up again, and Rachel jumped to her feet, anxious to change the subject. "I love this song! Let's dance!" She said, grabbing Jason's hands and pulling him up. The two wiggled and shimmied as they belted out the lyrics, and Rachel's worry melted away. When the song ended and the band took their final bows, Jason grabbed Rachel and spun her around, her face flying by in a whirlwind of happiness.

"You're coming to Hanson's party tomorrow, right?" Jason asked, hopefully.

"Sure, it sounds fun. What time should I be there? And where does he live?" Rachel was trying to decide if she could tell her mom about being invited to two different parties on Saturday or if she should just pretend she was spending the whole day at Reggie's.

Jason couldn't remember Hanson's address, but he gave her directions and Rachel hoped she could still remember them tomorrow. Indianapolis was a lot bigger than Allendale, where everybody knew where everything was. "I better get going." Her voice dropped. "My mom is probably waiting for me."

Jason pulled her in for one last goodbye kiss, scorching her lips with his blazing hot mouth as it overtook hers. She pulled away only when she felt herself about to implode from the heat. She turned and headed for the entrance to the park, hoping her face didn't show the ecstasy she felt. Her mother's car was waiting when she got to the fron,t and she shook herself back to reality and climbed in with an innocent smile plastered on.

"Did you have a nice time, sweetie?" Mary asked as Rachel buckled up.

"Yeah, it was great. Hey Mom, you know that group of friends I went to the movies with the other day? Well, they're all hanging out tomorrow. Do you think I could go? Would you take me?" Rachel quickly asked, wanting to avoid too many questions about tonight's activities.

"Sure, honey. I'd be happy to take you! I'm so glad you're making friends."

Sensing her mother's accommodating mood, Rachel decided to take the risk. She wasn't in the habit of lying to her mother, except, of course, for the huge revelation about Rider that she had kept secret for so long it didn't really seem like a lie, just a necessary omission. "And there's this other group that's getting together later... Do you think

I could go to that one, too?"

Mary's brows wrinkled and she gave Rachel a worried look. "That sounds like a pretty busy day…"

"I promise I'll get all my homework done beforehand… and my chores too!" Rachel begged.

"Okay, okay, I suppose," Mary conceded, a small smile on her face. She was incredibly happy that Rachel was fitting in. She often worried about her daughter's social life back in Michigan when the only person she ever seemed to connect with was Paige.

When the two arrived home, Rachel raced to her room to call her old bestie in private, psyched to tell her all about her amazing first date.

Chapter Thirteen

The Saturday morning sun poured demandingly through Rachel's bedroom window, reminding her she had a full day ahead of her. She groaned and stretched, wondering if she could still get her homework done in time if she slept just a little bit longer. Just then, her mother started up the vacuum cleaner downstairs, and Rachel knew she better get busy before her mom decided to add any more chores to her list. Mary seemed to think that if your current chores weren't enough motivation, a few more might help.

Rachel leaned out of the bed just far enough to hook her backpack and drag it into reach. She tried valiantly to focus on her algebra assignment, but algebra always made her think of Jason since he was in her class, and thoughts of Jason turned inexorably towards memories of last night's kisses and the amazing way her body tingled all over every time he touched her. A very distracted hour later, Rachel was finally finished with the assignment that should have only taken about 20 minutes. She quickly tidied her room just enough so that it would look okay if her mom walked by and headed for the shower.

Rider was in a peculiar mood that day. Last night's concert had been thrilling to him — the music, the dancing, the crowd of people. It was a very bizarre arrangement between him and Rachel. He had no control over her body, no way to express himself physically, but he could feel everything she felt and enjoy the sensations that coursed through her flesh. Rachel letting go of her body and giving over to pure emotion had been exhilarating for him. If he was honest with himself, he enjoyed the rush of ecstasy she felt every time Jason touched her, but his dislike for Jason was so overwhelming it distracted him from enjoying her pleasure, and he was loathe to admit he'd had a good time last night.

He was definitely excited about Reggie's party, though. Being with Rachel was great, but they didn't always have the same taste in entertainment, and sometimes he longed for more masculine forms of mental stimulation. A bunch of kooky people sitting around laughing at fart jokes sounded like a perfect Saturday to him.

On the other hand, though, he was dreading Hanson's party. He didn't understand why Rachel wanted to be with that crowd. They seemed self-centered and juvenile and completely void of redeeming qualities. They strutted around the school like invading warriors, convinced of their superiority and intent on the destruction of everyone else.

Rider thought Jason was a complete fraud, interested in Rachel only so long as he thought he could get something from her. Rider understood why Rachel was drawn to him, though. He knew her self-esteem was lacking, and

Jason said and did all the right things to make her feel special. He wished he could make her see how special she really was. He wished other people in her life had appreciated her the way he did.

When Rachel finished her shower, she sprayed some cleaner on the shower walls and threw on her robe to finish cleaning her bathroom. As she worked, she found herself humming the tunes then singing the words to her favorite songs from last night. Rider joined in her performance, and soon the two were belting out the words they remembered, making up the ones they didn't, and laughing hysterically at their complete lack of talent in either regard.

Rachel loved how she could always count on Rider to make everything fun. He could be grumpy occasionally, and his sarcasm sometimes made him seem like a scrooge, but deep down he was one of the happiest, most content people she'd ever known. Not a day went by that she didn't feel grateful for his company.

Her bathroom sparkling, Rachel pulled on some jeans and a flattering but comfy sweater, highlighted her features with a touch of blush, a few coats of mascara, and a swipe of lip gloss, and headed downstairs to find her mom.

Mary was in the kitchen drinking coffee and nibbling on some of her homemade pumpkin donut holes, so Rachel poured herself a glass of milk, popped a donut in her mouth, and joined her mother at the table.

"My room is picked up, my bathroom is clean, and my homework is done. Can I go to Reggie's now?" The cherubic look on her fresh, young face made her impossible to resist.

The protective mother instinct was niggling in the back of Mary's mind, but she couldn't really come up with a reason not to let Rachel go, so she nodded her assent, licked the cinnamon sugar crumbs from her fingers, finished her coffee, and grabbed her keys.

"Yay! Thank you, Mom, you're the best!" Rachel squealed and quickly tossed down the rest of her milk. "Can I take some pop over to Reggie's? I told them I'd bring some," she asked, pulling 2-liters from the fridge and shoving them into one of her mother's canvas grocery bags.

"You could've told me that before I went to the grocery store," Mary scolded lightly.

"Sorry, Mom. I didn't think. I'll leave a couple, okay?"

"You better, or your father will be a grouchy bear all day."

Rachel giggled at the mental image Rider created of her father in a bear costume, flashing shiny, white plastic fangs and claws, growling and chasing after her and his Mountain Dew. It was a pretty accurate comparison. Rachel imagined herself running in pseudo-terror from the Pop Monster as she lugged her bag to the car and quickly buckled in.

"What are you giggling about?" Mary wondered, a curious look on her face as she joined Rachel in the car.

"Oh just... nothing." Rachel grinned and focused her attention on programming Reggie's address into the GPS.

Twenty minutes later, they were pulling into an older, somewhat run-down neighborhood where the children rode their bikes up and down the streets to each other's houses, dropping them in the front lawns to join driveway basketball scrimmages and hopscotch contests. Mothers sat on concrete stoops in their pj's, watching the little ones, and dads raked leaves or worked under the hoods of their faded sedans. Rachel thought it looked homey, a little more welcoming than her neighborhood where everyone drove straight into their garages, and the kids played video games alone in their rooms.

Mary parked in front of Reggie's house and followed Rachel to the door, much to Rachel's chagrin. Their knock was immediately answered by a little boy in a Batman costume who pointed a light saber at Rachel and growled, "Arrr, who goes there?" in a pirate voice.

"Antwon, I done told you not to be answerin' that door!" A large woman in a flour-dusted apron came bustling out of the kitchen and shooed away the little superhero with a dishtowel. A smile lit up her face as she caught eyes with Rachel and Mary. "I'm LaShuana Williams," she announced brightly, unsuccessfully wiping her flour-covered hands on her apron before sticking one out for a handshake. Seeing the fruitlessness of her efforts, she shrugged her shoulders, laughed and dropped her dusty palms. "I'm cookin' up a mess a' wings for the young'uns, so you'll hafta pardon me," she begged. "You must be

Rachel. Ain't you a purdy thing! And you take after your momma, too," She said, nodding towards Mary with a happy smile.

"Thank you, LaShauna. It's so nice to meet you. I'm Mary Masterson," Mary said kindly, a pleased look on her face. Rachel could tell that Mrs. Williams had quelled any concerns her mother had about her hanging out at a stranger's house all day.

"Yo, Rachel!" hollered Reggie as he barreled down the hallway and leapt over the couch to grab her in a bear hug. "You made it!"

"Hi, Reggie," Rachel managed to squeak out of her collapsed lungs.

Realizing that Rachel's mother was standing behind her, Reggie quickly straightened up and stuck out his hand to greet her, his kamikaze entrance replaced with a respectful nod. "Thank you for bringin' her, Mizz Masterson. I'm Reggie."

"It's nice to meet you, Reggie." Mary smiled and shook his mammoth paw. "Thank you for inviting her. Rachel, just text me when you're ready to be picked up, okay? I have some errands to run so I'll be out and about all day."

"Okay thanks, Mom." Rachel reached out and gave her mom an impulsive hug goodbye.

Rachel handed Reggie her bag of soda after her mother had gone, and he carried it to the kitchen. Rachel followed him, enticed by the smell of bubbling oil and hot, crispy chicken wings slathered in BBQ sauce. "I thought you were serving your famous chicken wings, Reggie. These look like your momma's!" Rachel teased, sneaking a wing off the pile and nibbling on it gingerly, trying not to burn her tongue.

Before Reggie could form a good comeback, there was a quick knock on the door, and Garrett came sweeping in like a tornado, not waiting to be let in. He bellowed a greeting towards Reggie and slapped his hand in a high five before pouncing on the platter and shoving a steaming chicken wing straight into his mouth. His eyes popped open and his jaw dropped when the blazing hot meat touched his tongue, but he managed to keep it in his mouth and offered a garbled compliment of appreciation to Mrs. Williams who nodded and smiled knowingly and patted him on the back when he started to choke. When he could breathe again, he finally noticed Rachel and ran to her side, grabbing her in a sticky hug. Rachel chuckled as she lightly patted Garrett's head like she would a friendly dog's. "It's nice to see you, too, Garrett," Rachel offered, and realized it was surprisingly true. She had missed these goofy characters since she'd begun spending all her time with Jason.

Eve was next to arrive. She brought a platter of carrots and celery with dip and gave Rachel a happy smile when she saw her. Garrett found the supply of soda and began eagerly dumping ice into plastic cups and filling them to the top with his favorite fizzing elixir while Reggie carried the plate of wings to the living room. Rachel followed Eve to the couch and picked up the DVDs on the coffee table. "Have you ever seen any of these movies?" she asked her, scanning the cases.

"No, but Reggie has a knack for picking pretty good ones," Eve explained. "And the not-so-good ones are fun to mock, so we have a pretty good time, regardless."

Just then Tara arrived, on Tyler's arm no less, and the two had matching Cheshire grins, clearly an aftereffect from last night's activities. Her pan of brownies was slathered in thick chocolate frosting and sprinkled with nuts, and Tyler held a grocery bag full of different kinds of potato chips. Rachel was grateful she hadn't taken time to eat more of her mother's donuts, delicious as they were.

"So how was the concert last night?" Eve asked innocently but with a knowing look on her face. Her eyes connected briefly with Rachel's then settled curiously on Tara and Tyler who were sitting unusually close to each other on the love seat across the room.

"It was really good," Tara's face split in a silly grin. Tyler's perky smile indicated a similar opinion.

"Uh huh. Great music," Rachel elaborated. "Lots of people, everybody was dancing and having fun."

Eve's eyebrows raised in incredulity. "That's all? Great music and lots of fun? It seems to me like something more than just dancing happened last night."

"Oh, come on, Eve, you know a lady should never kiss and tell, right Tara?" Rachel hinted. Tara's eyes bugged out and she started to choke on her soda.

"Who said anything about kissing?" Tara sputtered.

"No one had to; it's all over your faces!" Eve answered with uncharacteristic sauciness.

"So, did you two ostriches finally dig your heads out of the sand enough to admit your feelings for each other?" Rachel asked bluntly with a devious smile.

"Wait a minute, wait a minute!" Garrett shrieked as he plopped down next to Tara and Tyler on the tiny love seat, his soda sloshing precariously close to the top of his cup. "You two like each other?"

The rest of the group moaned and chuckled at Garrett's obliviousness while Reggie reached to start the DVD. The afternoon passed quickly as the group rallied behind the nerd stars of the movies, and the snacks disappeared. Tara and Tyler stayed snuggled together on the sofa, exchanging doe-eyed glances, but Rachel barely thought of Jason, she was so caught up in the frivolity. She had practically forgotten her evening plans altogether when Jason texted her, offering her a ride to the party. Figuring her mom would probably appreciate less taxi duty, Rachel sent him Reggie's address and let her mom know she didn't have to pick her up.

Rachel could tell that Rider was bummed about leaving; he was totally in his element with this crowd. But the thought of seeing Jason again spurred all kinds of exciting emotions within Rachel, and she was eager to feel his touch. When the doorbell rang, she anxiously jumped to answer it. Rachel's face was beaming with happiness as she opened the door to Jason, but his sour expression quickly dimmed her smile.

"Rachel, wow, I didn't think I had the right address." Jason looked around cynically as he stepped into the living room. Reggie, Garrett and Tyler were engaged in an epic battle behind the sofa, and they hardly noticed Jason as they swung their toy light sabers wildly, barely missing Jason's head. Jason dodged their flailing weapons with a look of disgust and moved in for a kiss. "What's going on, Rachel? Why are all these people in your house?"

"Oh, this isn't my house, it's Reggie's," Rachel explained, "We're just hanging out, watching movies."

"Do you live in this neighborhood?" Jason asked, still skeptical, eyeing the others warily.

"No, I know Reggie from school. These are some of my friends." Eve and Tara waved politely from the sofa, and the boys paused their fighting just long enough to shout hello.

"Are you ready to get out of here?" Jason encouraged, not bothering to return a greeting to her friends.

"Sure, let me just grab the drinks." Rachel moved towards the kitchen to retrieve the leftover soda. Jason followed her. "Oh crap, they drank it all! I brought like 5 bottles! I was going to bring whatever was left to Hanson's," Rachel complained, seeing the horde of empty containers littering the counters.

Jason chuckled and turned Rachel back towards the

door. "Don't worry; I think there will be plenty of beverages."

Rachel waved goodbye to her friends and told Reggie thanks for inviting her as Jason guided her quickly out the door. His shiny Mazda looked out of place on the curb. Jason drove fast through the little neighborhood, and Rachel worried about the children playing near the road, but soon the streets got wider and less busy as the houses got larger and farther apart. Hanson's house was an elegant modern manse with a driveway as long as a city block that curved graciously from the street to the 3-car garage. Jason parked and popped open the trunk.

As Rachel rounded the back bumper, Jason lifted an access panel on the floor of the truck that hid the spare tire and a collection of half empty liquor bottles. "What is he, a traveling bartender?" Rider exclaimed, shock and disapproval in his tone.

"What's your pleasure?" Jason asked, plucking a clear bottle from the stash and waving his arm to indicate she should choose her favorite. Rachel stared dumbfounded at the bottles. Her parents rarely drank, and there was never liquor in the house. She didn't have a clue what most of them were. She felt uneasy at the thought of drinking again but didn't want to look like a prude in front of Jason, and she remembered how exhilarated she felt after a few swigs at the concert the night before. Grabbing randomly into the pile, she pulled out something with a peach on the front and handed it to Jason with a shy smile.

"Typical girl — likes the fruity drinks, huh?" Jason teased and stuck a few more bottles under his arms. He didn't bother knocking, just let himself in and headed straight for the kitchen. Zeke and Kyle were chugging beers, and Hanson was cheering them on. Zeke finished a millisecond before Kyle and declared his victory with a roar.

"Dude, just in time!" Hanson hollered when he saw Jason. "C'mon, you and me. Winner challenges Z for the championship!"

Jason eagerly pulled a can from the box on the counter and popped the tab. "On three — one, two, three!" He and Hanson threw their heads back simultaneously and began to pour the liquid down their throats. Jason beat Hanson and grabbed another beer to challenge Zeke.

Rachel wandered into the family room and saw Hannah, Lindsey, and Kelsey lounging on a large sectional sofa, sharing a joint and drinking something pink out of martini glasses. They always looked great at school, but their party clothes were amazing — not just high fashion, but extremely sexy as well. Rachel felt out of place in her sweater and jeans. They had a euphoric look on their faces, and although it didn't seem to be related to Rachel's entrance, it wasn't diminished by it either.

"Oohh, Jason brought his new toy!" Lindsey tittered and wiggled her fingers at Rachel. "Come join us, we were just talking about you!"

Rachel wasn't sure how to take that, but Lindsey's tone was innocent enough, so Rachel squeezed in between them on the sofa and tried to act confident. Their sweet, pungent smoke invaded her lungs, and she struggled not to cough.

"Yeah, we were just talking about how gorgeous your hair is, weren't we, girls?" Kelsey explained, running her fingers intimately through Rachel's waves. Rachel smiled hesitantly.

"Sooo soft and pretty," Hannah offered, leaning in to sniff Rachel's tresses. "Umm, smells like...peaches!" She giggled and lazily reached for her cocktail.

"Some of those skanks at our school have such ugly hair!" Kelsey criticized. "Why don't they just do something with it?"

"Yeah, like shave it off! That would look better than some of those hideous hairstyles they have now. Some of them just don't even try at all," Lindsey complained.

"I'm glad you're not ugly; it would be sooo much harder to be nice to you if you were," Kelsey announced, and the others giggled hysterically. Rachel hadn't had a lot of time to get to know these girls, but their behavior today seemed very different. They were usually too sophisticated to act silly.

"You seem really tense today, Rachie, like, totally stiff, you know?" Hannah cooed. "Maybe you just need some candy to help you relax!" Just then, Rachel noticed a baggie on the table filled with several different kinds of pills and tablets. Hannah grabbed the baggie and held it up, dangling it in front of Rachel. "The orange ones are my favorite, but you can try them all if you want!"

Rachel's heart fluttered as she stared at the bag of "candy." Drugs seemed like something only the people in movies did, usually with disastrous results. But these were the coolest girls in the whole school, and they acted like it was no big deal. They didn't look like pathetic losers like the druggies on TV did. They looked fabulous, and they acted like they were having a great time. Rachel envied their relaxed confidence. Did she dare? What was the worst that could happen?

"You could overdose, or do something stupid and end up hurting yourself, that's what!" Rider exclaimed. "Since when did drugs become an acceptable form of recreation for us? The alcohol is bad enough, but this is just stupid, Rachel! What if your parents find out? We need to get out of here. These are not our kind of people. Go back to Reggie's and eat some more brownies. There's enough sugar in those to give you a natural high."

"You're right, Rider, these aren't our kind of people. They are cooler than we've ever been! And I want to fit in with them. Especially since I'm with Jason now. I'm not going to overdose, I'm just going to try one pill. It will wear off by the time we go home, anyway. My parents will never even know," Rachel retorted, irritated at Rider's authoritarian attitude. He was not the boss of her, and she didn't like his condescending tone.

With just the barest hint of reluctance, Rachel took the baggie from Hannah and selected a bright blue tablet. She hoped no one noticed the slight quivering of her fingers as she brought the pill to her lips. Kelsey held out her martini glass, and Rachel quickly washed down the pill with a big gulp of the bittersweet liquid. A huge smile spread across her face as she realized she had just done the most reckless thing she'd ever done in her whole life and it felt amazing.

Lindsay squealed as a new song came on the radio, and she popped up excitedly. "Oh, this is my favorite! Let's dance, girls!" She grabbed a remote to turn up the volume till Adam Levine's sexy howls reverberated off the walls. The others rolled their eyes but climbed off the couch and joined her, and a few moments later they were all singing along as they shimmied and swayed to the pounding beat.

Rachel felt a little embarrassed by her ragtag appearance compared with their shimmery party wear, but she soon lost herself in the music as the magic blue pill worked its way into her system. Her limbs became liquid as her joints relaxed, and her mind loosened its grip on her inhibitions. She felt carefree and happy, and she couldn't remember why she'd ever worried about anything other than this moment of pleasure. Even Rider lost his patronizing edge and began to enjoy himself.

The boys heard the commotion and soon joined the girls in the living room, gawking in lustful appreciation as the girls writhed. When the music slowed down, the boys joined the dance, taking advantage of the girls' uninhibitedness to grope and fondle them as they ground their hips against theirs and sucked hungrily at their throats. One by one, the couples retreated to bedrooms for more privacy till only Rachel and Jason were left in the living room.

Jason pulled Rachel down to the couch and began to kiss her like a man staking a claim on his property. His kisses left a blaze of fire as his lips caressed her collarbone, the hollow of her neck, and finally her lips, capturing her skin with his teeth before thrusting his tongue into her mouth. His body was heavy on hers as he laid her down on the sofa, trapping her between his muscular arms. A niggling in the back of her mind tried to remind her to stop and think about what she was doing, but the sensations coursing through her body muffled the sound of her conscience and Rider's voice.

A trilling noise finally broke through her trance, and a few beats later Rachel realized it was the phone in her pocket, playing a warning siren. The fog of passion separated as Rachel recognized her mother's ringtone, and she struggled to push Jason away so she could sit up.

"Where are you, Rachel? It's late and I want you safe at home before I go to bed. Tell me the address and I'll be there to pick you up," her mother demanded as she answered the phone. Glancing around the room at the beer bottles, wine glasses, and illegal intoxicants, Rachel could only imagine the disastrous reaction her mother would have if she walked in and saw what they'd been doing.

"NO! I mean, there's no need, Mom. I was, on my way home anyway. I'll be in bed before you are, I promise," Rachel stammered, desperate to sound calm and normal instead of high and jittery like she felt.

"I have to go home, Jason, my mom is worried,"

Rachel said apologetically as she ended the call.

"But we're finally alone! Can't you tell her you need a few more minutes?" Jason pleaded, teasing her breasts with the tips of his fingers and leaning in for a kiss.

"This doesn't have to be our last date, does it?" Rachel asked, simultaneously leaning into his waiting lips and pushing him back with her hands. The interruption had cleared her head enough to make her realize she wasn't sure she wanted to go all the way just yet, but it was so hard to say no to his seductive persuasion. Although he was quiet, Rachel could sense Rider's similar emotion as well. He didn't like that it was Jason who was touching her, but the passion coursing through her body was a pleasure more intense than any he had never known.

"When can I see you again?" Jason caressed her neck and shoulders, a hungry look in his eyes.

"We see each other every day at school, silly!" Rachel teased, experiencing the power of her feminine wiles for the first time. It seemed like she held Jason in the palm of her hand, so easily manipulated by a flirtatious wink or a sultry gaze.

"You know that's not what I mean!" Jason pleaded, a look of desperation on his face. "Are you free tomorrow?"

"Maybe; I'll have to get permission. I was gone all day, so my parents might not let me," Rachel explained. She really did want to spend more time with him. She had never had many friends before, and never a boyfriend, so her parents weren't used to her going out so much.

Jason wrapped his arm around her waist, and the two stumbled to the car, kissing and groping hungrily, unwilling to let an inch of space come between their bodies. Jason walked Rachel to the passenger side and opened the door for her. His breath smelled strongly of alcohol as he awkwardly guided her into her seat and gave her one more desperate kiss. Rachel wondered briefly if he was too intoxicated to drive, but he seemed clear-headed, if a little clumsy, and in her rush to get home she could think of no better option.

Jason chattered anxiously as he slowly backed out of the driveway, overcompensating for the gradual curve and weaving erratically back and forth across the pavement and into the lawn. When he finally reached the end of the drive, Rachel was relieved to see there was no oncoming traffic and he was able to successfully back out into the road. She relaxed as his driving straightened and steadied as they made their way through the near-empty streets of Hanson's neighborhood.

"So there's a basketball game tomorrow, and afterward all the guys usually go out to celebrate, or commiserate, and I was thinking maybe you could go with me, if you want to?" Jason offered, a hopeful look in his eyes.

That actually sounded pretty good to Rider. He'd never been to a basketball game before, only watched bits and pieces of them on TV, but the fast-paced tempo, the pounding of the ball as the players raced from one end of the court to the other, the crowds stomping their feet in the bleachers, and the energetic chants of the cheerleaders shouting out encouragements seemed exciting to him. Plus, hanging out afterward meant getting to enjoy a little guy time. He didn't know many of the other players, but he was hopeful that their personalities were less obnoxious than Jason's. Rachel didn't quite share Rider's enthusiasm for the invitation but she would take any opportunity to be with Jason.

"That sounds fun," she replied as genuinely as possible, a warm smile lighting her face. "Hey, turn here!" Rachel screeched as Jason drove past her road, oblivious to everything but her as he gazed into her eyes.

Eyes still on Rachel, Jason did not notice the oncoming car as he swerved to the left in response to her warning. With a shriek of metal, the two vehicles smashed into a space the size of one, the force of the impact catapulting the teens from their seats and sending them crashing through the windshield. Their bodies bounced and tumbled onto the road, landing in broken heaps several feet in front of the car.

Chapter Fourteen

Rider feels the jarring impact of the collision and the sense of weightlessness as Rachel's body flies through the air. He sees the windshield shatter around Rachel's head and hears the rush of wind as she sails through the broken window into the cool night air, limbs flailing uselessly. His mind recoils at the intense pain as her bones crumple beneath her on the cement, flesh bruised and torn and bleeding, the blood collecting around her in a warm, sticky pool. Her eyes are closed so he can't see where they are, but he feels the cold ground beneath them and hears voices nearby, anxious with fear and worry. His mind races as he tries to comprehend what happened, and he reaches out to Rachel to make sense of the confusion, but she is not there.

Her consciousness is turned off, like a movie suddenly gone black, and at first he's not sure if she's still alive at all. In a panic, he cries her name over and over, frantically trying to rouse her from her silence. He thrashes and screams inside her, desperate for some response from her lifeless body, till he falters in exhaustion, only to find his assurance in the silence, the quiet thrum of her still-beating heart.

She's still alive! He thinks in instantaneous relief as his heart swells in time to the beating of hers. He couldn't imagine what would happen to him if she died, but he doesn't give a thought to his own mortality, only hers. He realizes she must be unconscious, not dead, but her wounds could still be life-threatening. Where's Jason? Why isn't he helping? Is he unconscious too? He wonders, wishing hopelessly for Rachel's eyes to open so he could see.

The faint sound of sirens in the background comforted Rider, assuring him that help was on the way. Their ear-piercing wail grew louder as they approached, and Rider nervously awaited their arrival, desperately hoping it wasn't too late. The ambulance stopped several yards from where Rachel lay, and Rider could hear the EMTs jump from the cab and begin talking rapidly. "Over here!" he tried yelling, but his voice had no mouth, and no one could hear his frantic call. Finally, he heard the sound of approaching footsteps as the voices grew closer, gruff and urgent.

He felt her body, limp and broken, being lifted carefully onto a stretcher, the straps pulled tight against her fragile form. They carried her slowly to the waiting ambulance and one of the men inserted an IV as the van began to move.

"Don't worry, darlin', we're gonna take good care of you," the EMT assured them, gently smoothing her hair. The ride to the hospital was mercifully short, and soon the doors were opened and Rachel was quickly transferred to a gurney and swarmed by doctors and nurses. One woman in particular seemed to be in charge, and she barked out orders for tests and treatments as the EMTs rattled off a description of Rachel's injuries that was filled with words incomprehensible to Rider. Their brusque tone and the sheer litany of symptoms indicated that Rachel's condition was severe, and Rider wished that he could understand them.

"Here comes the second one," someone shouted as the hospital doors opened and another victim's injuries were called out with medical detachment. Rider wondered if they were talking about Jason or someone from the other car. He didn't get a chance to find out before Rachel's gurney was whisked away, and the staff began poking and prodding her body, assessing the damage.

"She's going to need surgery to reduce the pressure on her brain if she has any chance of surviving this," Rider heard the doctor say. "Let's get her into CT."

Rider rode a wave of fear and panic as the doctors scanned Rachel's battered body and prepped her for surgery. Her unresponsiveness was terrifying to him. She lay limp and silent as they cut away her clothes, shaved a line through her beautiful hair, and locked her head in a metal trap that looked more like a torture device than a surgical instrument. How could she not feel this? He wondered. Where is she? Is she even still in here? He'd never felt so cut off from her before. Even in sleep, her mind was a constant presence, filled with dreams and the random wisps of thought that perpetuated her slumber. This silence felt like death to him, but he had to believe it wasn't. The doctors seemed grim, but still hopeful. He hoped desperately that their urgent willingness to operate meant they believed she could still be saved.

The sounds of brain surgery were fascinating but torturous to Rider. He could hear the sharp clink of the metal instruments rattling against each other on the tray as the doctor barked out their names imperiously, the sharp slice of the scalpel through Rachel's tender flesh, the moist slurp of the suction as it sucked away her spilling blood, the high-pitched whine of the drill as it bore a hole in Rachel's skull, and the terse voices of the doctors and nurses, their professional jargon a meaningless jumble of frightening words. Only one sound provided any comfort to Rider – the steady beat of the heart monitor, faithfully assuring everyone in the room that Rachel's mangled body was still fighting to stay alive. When the harsh sounds of surgery became overwhelming to him, Rider clung to the soothing rhythm of Rachel's heart, beating out a promise that she would come back to him.

A simple stutter of the machine was all it took to shatter Rider's faith, and the frantic announcement that Rachel's heart was in distress sent him free-falling into an abyss of pain and despair. The doctors and nurses jumped into action, their attentions immediately diverted from Rachel's head to her heart. Above their shouts and the clatter of equipment, Rider could hear Rachel's heart faltering even as they tried frantically to stabilize it. A deafening squeal from the monitor drowned out every other noise as Rachel's heart stopped and the erratic spikes on the screen became a flat line.

As Rider realized the life had left Rachel's body, his heart began to drown in a sea of crushing agony, but concern for his own fate suddenly took over his mind as he felt his soul being ripped from her corpse. His spirit lifted away from her body, and for the first time, he saw her form from the outside. She looked as small and helpless as a little child, only her head and neck sticking out from a crumpled layer of surgical draping. The doctors and nurses hovered over her, desperately trying to revive her lifeless body.

Shutting out the petrifying realization of his own demise, Rider took one last moment to mourn for Rachel. His best friend, his constant companion, truly his soulmate, Rachel had been one half of his soul. As the distance between them grew farther, Rider felt as if he was being torn in two, and with his last thought he wondered if he and Rachel really were two separate souls inhabiting one body or perhaps just one soul, with an inexplicable fissure creating two consciousnesses.

Next door in Surgery Room 2, a boy named Cameron Wilson lay with his chest cut open on the operating table as doctors tried to repair the critical damage caused by the accident. His heart was strong — in the prime of youth and robust from the intense exercise of high school athletics, but the force of the collision had ripped apart the muscle like an old pair of jeans, and the doctors were working feverishly to mend it when his soul lost its grip on his body and he left this world for the next.

Highly trained in modern resuscitation methods and unwilling to accept the end of a life so short and full of promise, the doctors in Surgery Rooms 1 & 2 ignored the screaming siren of their patients' heart monitors and all the signs indicating death and worked desperately to restart their hearts and breathe life back into their adolescent bod-

Soulmate

ies.

Cameron Wilson was the first to die, his soul vacating his body, leaving an empty shell, but the doctors continued resuscitation efforts way past the point of realistic recovery, pumping his heart by hand and forcing air into his lungs in the futile hope he would revive.

In the room next door, Rachel Masterson's death was less fatal, if there can be such a thing, because her soul had barely reached the limits of the arena when it was pulled back forcefully into her body. The surgeons and nurses breathed a tandem sigh of relief as her heart began to beat again, a steady rhythm that calmed their panic and allowed their attention to return to her open brain.

Chapter Fifteen

A week after Rachel's accident, Paige Donovan was lounging awkwardly with her legs dangling over the armrest of a stiff hospital chair next to Rachel's bed when the cute boy in the next bed woke up. Rachel was taking a Cosmo quiz called, "How Sexy Is Your Body Language?" when Cameron croaked out a snarky comment. Technically, Paige was taking the quiz for Rachel, since Rachel was still annoyingly comatose, but Paige knew Rachel well enough to answer all the questions for her, probably more honestly than Rachel would answer them herself, so she was pretty confident of the results when she declared that Rachel's body language was "Sweetly Sexy a la Taylor Swift."

"Coma Boy" as Paige liked to call him, had been a perfectly-vegetative roommate for the similarly-unconscious Rachel since they both escaped the clutches of the afterlife during emergency surgery following their collision the week before. The doctors acted optimistic that both of them might recover, but so far Paige hadn't seen much sign of life from either one of them since she got here late Friday night. She had spent the entire week begging her parents to pull her out of school so she could come see Rachel, but had succeeded only in convincing them to drive her down for the weekend. Since then, she had been camped out next to Rachel's bed, reading her amusing magazine articles, gossiping about the kids they both knew, and casting surreptitious glances at the hunky hottie in the nearby cot.

"What did you say?" Paige sputtered, practically falling out of her chair in surprise.

"I said drool isn't sexy or sweet, it's just disgusting," Cameron replied with a jaunty smile on his face.

"Speak for yourself, Coma Boy." Paige popped a hand on her hip. "She may be drooling, but you've been farting every five minutes since I got here! VERY sexy."

Cameron chuckled at her snappy response, only slightly embarrassed that he had been passing gas in front of such a lovely young lady, voluntarily or not.

"I can't believe the first thing you did when you woke up from a coma was make a sarcastic comment about the girl you almost killed. Actually, I can't believe you even woke up. I thought you were a goner for sure," Paige retorted.

"I almost killed her? What happened?" Cameron face contorted into a mask of guilt and horror.

"You don't remember?" Paige asked curiously, plopping down in the chair next to Cameron's bed.

"No, I, I don't remember... anything..." Cameron's voice dwindled to an anxious whisper. "Who am I? How did I get here? What happened to me? And to her?" The terror on his face grew as he searched deeper for memories but came up empty.

"Whoa," Paige jolted. "Like, you don't even remember who you are? Like, amnesia or something? That is SO freaky!" Cameron's pained expression made Paige realize the inappropriateness of her comment.

"Sorry, I'm an idiot, I know," Paige apologized, biting her lip, her hands fluttering uselessly. "I can't really help you much. I mean, I know your name's Cameron, cuz that's what your parents and the doctors call you, and I know you were in a head-on collision with my friend Rachel here a week ago, landing you both in the hospital for some seriously major surgery — brain surgery for her and heart surgery for you. And I know you both almost bought it on the operating table, but the doctors brought you both back — pretty freaky, huh?"

Cameron blinked in surprise at Paige's explanation. Something about her story seemed kind of familiar, but at the same time not. The name Cameron didn't ring any bells whatsoever. How could he not recognize his own name? And the idea of him driving seemed completely foreign, too. Yet, the accident seemed familiar somehow. He didn't really remember the details, more like the feelings. He remembered shock and pain and the feeling of hopelessness. And why did he feel like he knew this sassy girl with curly black hair?

"You said my parents call me Cameron. Where are

they?" Cameron asked anxiously, hoping their faces would jog his memory. This feeling of ignorance about his own life was starting to overwhelm him. Would his memory ever come back? And what if it didn't? The past was like a huge black hole that threatened to suck him in when he looked too deeply into it.

"They left a little bit ago to get something to eat from the cafeteria. They've been here most of the afternoon. They seem like nice people. And they sure think the world of you! Geez, you'd think you were God's gift to mankind the way they talk about you! They're all like — Cameron, we loooooovvve you. Cameron, we miii-iiiiissss you. Cameron, we can't wait to look into your beautiful blue eyes again!" Paige flung out her arms and threw back her head for dramatic effect, then topped it off with kissy noises. Cameron just rolled his eyes at her when she finally dropped the act.

"Thanks for the replay. At least I'll know what to expect when they get back," Cameron retorted, grinning. He hated to admit it, but he kind of liked this little pip-squeak of a girl. Her sarcasm made him laugh, and it helped take the edge off his anxiety.

"So tell me about your friend," Cameron urged, hoping to take his mind off his own worries. The girl didn't know him, so her story probably couldn't shed any light on his lost memories, but he owed her at least the courtesy of asking about her.

"Hmmm, where to begin." Paige tapped her lip with a thoughtful look. "Well, Rachel here is my best friend, has been since kindergarten. I'm Paige, by the way..."

"Nice to meet you, Paige. I'm Cameron," he replied with a grin. "Or at least that's what they tell me."

"Ha ha. ANYWAY..." Paige continued, "We lived in Michigan, but Rachel's dad got transferred a few weeks ago, and he moved their family down here to Indianapolis, which TOTALLY ruined everything, but that's another story I guess." Paige sighed as she thought about how miserable she'd been without Rachel since then.

"Of course, Rachel fared a little better than I have, I guess, cuz she made a whole bunch of new friends, including a super-hot boyfriend, or so she said, anyway. She never did send me that pic she promised...." Paige's voice faltered as her thoughts drifted.

"So, what do you know about the accident?" Cameron prodded, seeing Paige's mind wander. He wasn't interested in the super-hot boyfriend.

"Well, I guess she had gone to a party with her boyfriend. According to the doctors there were some... illegal substances involved, but I just can't believe that. I mean, Rachel has never done any of that stuff!"

Cameron felt a twinge of relief at her admission. Maybe the accident wasn't all his fault. His rapt attention urged Paige to go on.

"So anyway, her boyfriend, Jason, was driving her home when the accident happened. I guess they weren't wearing seat belts or something because they both went through the windshield. Rachel's head swelled up like a balloon, and they had to cut open her skull to relieve the pressure. They still don't know if she'll be okay or not, or if she'll ever wake up." Paige's expression grew dark as she contemplated that possibility. "But she's a fighter, you know? And she HAS to be okay, she just has to. Besides, you woke up, and other than being a little scrambled, you don't seem brain dead or anything. Right?" Paige teased, a weak smile on her face. Humor was always her outlet for stressful situations.

Despite Paige's attempt at levity, Cameron couldn't manage a smile. Paige's optimism might be a little unrealistic. Brain injuries were really serious, and if there was much chance of her recovering at all, she probably would have woken up already. It didn't sound like there was much hope for Rachel. He didn't even know the girl, but the thought of her dying made him immeasurably sad. Survivor's guilt, he supposed. Could he really have ruined the life of this young girl with a simple accident? Was this tragedy all his fault?

"What about me?" Cameron whispered painfully. "Was I... intoxicated?" He didn't remember if he was that kind of guy or not.

"No, I don't think so," Paige offered gently. "It sounds like Jason must have swerved in front of you, so I don't think the police are putting the blame on you."

The police?! Cameron shuddered. What if they charged me with this? Could I go to jail? What if the girl dies? Would they consider that manslaughter? Cameron imagined spending the rest of his life behind bars for an accident he didn't even remember. All of a sudden he realized he hadn't heard the whole story.

"What about the boyfriend? Where's he? Is he okay?" Cameron begged for it to be true. One look at Paige's face and he knew it wasn't.

"He... didn't make it," Paige whispered, her head bent so low he could barely hear her. Cameron's face froze in horror as the weight of a human life fell on his shoulders. A boy was dead because of him! He began to hyperventilate as the reality of the situation overtook him, and he clenched the sheets between his fingers.

"Dude, don't freak out!" Paige wailed, rushing to comfort the boy. She sat gingerly on the edge of his bed and tried to soothe him, her hands flapping uncertainly then eventually taking his head in her hands and pulling him against her. He sobbed into her chest as she smoothed his hair and rocked him gently back and forth, whispering assurances into his ear.

When the Wilsons returned a few moments later, they were shocked to find their previously-comatose son awake and sobbing and wrapped in the arms of a strange girl. Their expressions flashed like comic strip caricatures from surprise to delight to concern as they took in the scene.

"Cameron!" Mrs. Wilson squealed as she ran to his bedside. "You're awake! I'm so happy! But what's wrong, darling?"

Paige released Cameron at the sound of his mother's

voice and jumped guiltily off his bed. "I'm sorry, Mrs. Wilson. It's my fault he's upset." Paige smoothed her shirt over her hips and tugged on a curl.

"What happened? How long has he been awake? Why didn't you call us?!" Mrs. Wilson's voice and distress level rose with each successive question.

"It's okay, Janice. We've only been gone for a few minutes. Let's just be grateful our boy is finally awake." Mr. Wilson's voice was soft and nonjudgmental.

"He doesn't remember anything, so I was telling him what happened," Paige explained awkwardly.

"Oh, darling, I'm sure it must be a shock to you to wake up in the hospital all alone!" Mrs. Wilson cooed, embracing her son. Cameron knew he should feel something for these people he assumed were his parents, but they felt like total strangers to him. He felt more comfortable in Paige's embrace than he did in his mother's.

Mrs. Wilson felt her son stiffen in her arms, and she pulled back to look at him. His face was a study in angst as he tried to process all his emotions. "Everything's going to be all right, sweetheart. We're here now, and you're going to be fine."

"He doesn't remember who you are," Paige mumbled uncomfortably.

"What?" Mrs. Wilson gawked. "Of course he knows who we are! We're his parents, for heaven's sake!" She looked closely into Cameron's eyes, trying to discern recognition. She saw only fear and confusion. "Cameron? You recognize your momma, don't you?"

Cameron was saved from answering by the sudden arrival of the nurse who tittered happily upon seeing him sitting up and flitted around his bed checking his vitals and making perky comments as she recorded his status in his chart. "Oh, you must be so relieved to have your son back!" she exclaimed as she shined a light into Cameron's eyes to check for pupil dilation. It was then that she noticed the apprehension written on his face and swirling around the occupants of the room. "Let's get the doctor in here to have a little look-see, okay?" She quickly exiting the room in search of someone higher up to take over.

Meanwhile, Mrs. Wilson resumed her motherly ministrations while Paige looked on in morbid curiosity. This helpless boy and his distraught parents were not her problem, but she couldn't help but be fascinated by their situation. She wondered which was more terrifying — to forget your own memories or to have the person you love forget you. Paige decided they'd probably like to deal with this in private, so she whispered a goodbye to Rachel and quietly left the room. Her parents were back at Rachel's house visiting with the Mastersons, so Paige texted a request for a ride and headed to the lobby to wait.

Her mind filled the empty time by imagining increasingly scary scenarios about Rachel's recovery. Would she ever wake up? And if she did, would she be as lost as Cameron was? What if she had brain damage that turned her into a vegetable? Paige couldn't imagine a world without Rachel. Even though she was far away now, at least they could still text and call and occasionally visit. What if she could never talk to her friend again? Never complain to her about her awful day at school or compare notes about the cute boys they knew? Paige couldn't stand to even think about it any longer. She would stay hopeful and positive until the day Rachel woke up and called her a dumb name for even imagining such dreadful possibilities. Just then, her parents drove up and she put on a happy face, eager to share the good news that Rachel's roommate was awake.

Chapter Sixteen

Almost two weeks had passed since Rachel's accident when Paige got a happy call from Rachel's mom, announcing that she was finally waking up. It didn't happen all of a sudden like it did for Coma Boy, one minute dead to the world and the next wide awake and making sarcastic comments to total strangers. Rather, it started with a simple mutter, random words whispered anxiously as her eyes fluttered beneath her lids. Mary tried to stimulate her daughter to full awareness, but only managed to get a wiggle out of one of her fingers the first day. The next day, Rachel opened her eyes a few times, but she didn't respond when her parents tried to talk to her. Mary worried her brain had suffered too much trauma to ever be normal again, but the doctor assured her a full recovery was still possible, so Mary and Rob waited patiently by their daughter's bedside, hoping and praying their daughter was still alive somewhere inside.

Mary had helped to persuade Paige's mother Cathy to bring her down again for the weekend, in hopes that her presence would stimulate Rachel to awaken. Her hope turned to desperation on Friday when Rachel finally came to full awareness. She awoke, not with the sudden joy that Mary experienced when she first saw her daughter react to stimulation, or even with the temporary confusion her doctor had prepared them to expect, but with a frantic terror so raw and inexplicable that Rob and Mary could only pray their daughter's friend could help to ease Rachel's distress.

Mary called Cathy Donovan's cell phone number, hoping to speed their arrival, as she alternated between unsuccessfully comforting her traumatized daughter and trying to understand what had her so upset. Rachel had awoken late Friday afternoon with a scream in her throat, and since then her pleas for help had continued unabated.

"Where's Rider?" she had cried as her body jerked awake and she bolted up in bed, searching the room in fear and confusion. "What happened to him?!"

"It's okay, sweetie. You're all right," Mary had answered reassuringly, rushing to her daughter's side and taking her head in her hands. "You've had an accident and you're in the hospital, but Mommy's right here now, and so is Daddy, and you're going to be all right."

"But he's gone, Mom! Where is he? What happened to him?! I can't find him!" Rachel was unconsolable. So many years had passed since Rachel had mentioned the imaginary friend she called Rider that Mary had forgotten all about the stories she used to tell about the little boy who lived in her head.

"Who's Rider, sweetheart? Is he one of your new

friends? You were with someone named Jason when you had the accident." Mary was angry at first when she learned from a stranger that her daughter had a boyfriend she didn't know about, and she was filled with rage when she learned his intoxication was the likely cause of their fateful crash. But her fury turned to sadness when Jason succumbed to the severity of his injuries, and her sympathy for the mother who had lost her teenage son overwhelmed her initial desire for revenge.

Rachel's parents tried helplessly to determine who Rachel was talking about. A few of her friends from school had visited, but no one named Rider as far as they knew. With Rob and Mary unable to settle Rachel's panic, Rachel began to beg for Paige, and Mary was hopeful Paige could shed light on the mystery that had Rachel so agitated.

"Cathy, it's Mary. Are you on the road? Rachel's awake and she's asking for Paige." She tried to hide her anxiety, but it was evident to Cathy that Mary was in distress.

"That's wonderful news!" Cathy exclaimed, hoping to brighten Mary's emotions. "We should be there in another hour. Maybe Paige could talk to Rachel on the phone?"

"Yes, yes, let's try that." Mary sighed in relief, handing the phone to Rachel. "Here, honey, you can talk to Paige on the phone till she gets here."

"Paige?" Rachel squeaked out a desperate query.

"Hey, dork face! It's about time you woke up, you

big loser! Do you know how boring it is to talk to some-body in a coma?"

"Rider's gone, Paige!" Rachel sobbed, ignoring Paige's attempt at humor, her grief too intense for levity.

"What do you mean, Rach?"

"He's just... gone! I can't hear him, I can't feel him. I can't find him anywhere! What if I killed him, Paige?! What if he's gone forever?" Rachel's shrieks rose higher and higher till her voice peaked and fell and her cries crumbled into heaving sobs.

"Whoa, calm down, Rach." Paige tried to keep her tone calm and even. "Maybe he's just still out of it, like you were. Like a coma or something. Or maybe it's the medicine you're taking that's shut him out. I'm sure you're on like some heavy duty pain meds, right? Those things could knock out a horse! Hey, maybe you've discovered a way to finally shut him up once in a while, just take some prescription pain meds and, voila, peace and quiet for a few hours!"

"Yeah, maybe you're right." Rachel sighed, a wave of relief flooding her body. Her whole body relaxed and her countenance softened as she considered Paige's expla-nation. For the first time since she woke, a small smile cracked her anxious face.

Mary still didn't know what Rachel was talking about, but she was just pleased to see Rachel's terror abated. She sank down into the chair next to her husband and breathed a sigh of relief as Rachel chatted happily with her friend. She knew there were more hard conversations to have, but for now, her daughter was alive and awake, and that was all that mattered.

"So you missed out on seeing the hottie in the bed next to you all last week," Paige offered saucily. "He was the boy in the car that hit you. I spent half the day last Saturday staring at him since you were such lousy company, and then he woke up and I got to talk to him. Pretty cool guy, kinda funny. Reminded me of Rider, actually."

"Oh my gosh, Paige! I didn't even think about him! Was he okay? What about Jason?"

"Uhhhh," Paige stammered, searching for words. "Maybe you ought to talk to your mom about that..."

"Why? Is it bad? Paige, what do you know?" Rachel demanded, the tension returning like a monsoon, flooding her with apprehension.

"Rachel, let me talk to Paige for a second, sweetheart," Mary requested, taking the phone from her daughter's shaking hands. "Paige? Let me talk to Rachel now, okay? We'll see you soon." She ended the call and turned to face her distraught daughter.

"Mom? What happened to the boy I was riding with? Is he okay?" Rachel's voice shook with fear.

"I'm sorry, sweetheart, but Jason didn't make it. He was hurt too badly," Mary explained with sorrow in her voice.

"What do you mean, 'He didn't make it?' " A look

of horror twisted her face.

"His injuries were too severe, honey. He died shortly after the accident. There was nothing they could do."

Rachel covered her face with her hands as great wracking sobs took over her body. Rob and Mary comforted their daughter as best as they could, but neither had any words of hope to ease her pain.

Chapter Seventeen

6 weeks after the accident, her body had healed and her pain abated enough for Rachel to return to high school to finish out her sophomore year. Thanks to weekly visits from her science club friends, Rachel had managed to keep up with most of her school work and the local gossip, but the thought of all those piteous looks and questioning faces had Rachel dreading her return. Would they blame her for Jason's death? Would they wish he had survived instead of her?

And what about Cameron? She had learned from Tara that Cameron was a student at Indy High whose return had been met with surprise and confoundment since his memory loss left him a markedly different person than who he once was. He didn't remember the friends who had anxiously awaited his arrival, nor did he appreciate their attempts to revive the person he once was with their not-so-subtle hints that the new Cameron was inferior to the old. Rachel felt terrible about his condition, but at least he was alive and healthy. The guilt of Jason's death weighed much heavier on her conscience.

Worse than the humiliating shame of her bad choices, or the guilt over Cameron's memory loss, or the stinging pain of Jason's death, worse than any of that was the fact that Rider was gone.

The first few days, Rachel clung desperately to Paige's explanation that Rider was just still recovering from the accident, but deep down she knew it wasn't true. Rider had no body in need of recuperation, no brain suppressed by swelling. Rider was a just a soul, taking residence where it shouldn't, and Rachel's trauma had evicted him. She never imagined a world where she survived and he didn't, but somehow her heart kept beating despite the fact that he was gone. Every breath ached with the loss of him. Rachel wasn't sure what she believed about the afterlife, but she had to hope that Rider lived on somewhere and perhaps someday she would be with him again. Any other possibility was too unbearable to contemplate.

Rachel boarded the number 10 bus to Indy High the first Monday after spring break with a carefully crafted hairdo covering the shaved spot on her head, but her face couldn't disguise the jumbled mess of emotions inside. She had spent the last seven days hanging out with Paige whose parents had been willing to let her visit since she was out of school for the holiday. The two had talked and laughed and gossiped till most of Rachel's worries disappeared, but they had returned in excess at Paige's departure. Rachel's apprehension eased somewhat at the sight of Tara, a welcoming smile on her face and an empty spot on the seat next to her, as usual.

"Well, look who deigned to grace us with her presence!" Tara patted the bench and reached out to hug Rachel as she took her seat. "This bus ride has been sooooo interminably boring without you!"

"I know, I'm the life of the party, aren't I?" Rachel twisted her lips in a weak smile. "Or should I say the death of it?" A look of sorrow shadowed her face.

"Don't talk like that; it wasn't your fault. Everybody will be glad to see you," Tara assured her. "In fact, I think Garrett has a present for you!"

Rachel cringed at the thought. Garrett's unrequited crush had only deepened with Rachel's absence, according to Tara, and Rachel wasn't sure how to fend him off without hurting his feelings.

As the girls entered the school, Rachel's eyes couldn't help but be drawn to the elaborate memoriam for Jason set up in the lobby. There were cards and balloons and stuffed animals crowding a table erected under a large print of Jason's last yearbook photo. In it, his green eyes sparkled with life and happiness, a barely disguised laugh behind his movie-star smile. Rachel's eyes welled up with tears that she didn't bother to contain as her fingers reached to caress his glossy paper cheek.

Tara put her arm around Rachel's shoulder and muttered "I'm sorry" in her ear as other students began to encircle them. Rachel ignored their sorrowful murmurs and whispered condolences as she focused all her attention on remembering Jason and how he made her feel. Maybe he had been a bad influence on her as her parents were quick to point out, his reckless choices endangering her life and costing him his, but she couldn't bring herself to regret the time she spent with him and the passion he had awakened in her, even though the loss of him was made that much greater because of it.

She had missed his funeral, lying comatose in the hospital, but this simple display confirmed the reality of his death and released in her a grief more intense than she had ever felt before. The guilt and pain of Cameron's injury, Jason's death, and Rider's departure swirled around her like a flood, knocking the strength from her body and engulfing her with sorrow. Her knees trembled as she struggled to stay upright, and Tara's arms supported her as she led her to a nearby bench.

"I'm sorry, Rachel. I know how much he meant to you," Tara consoled.

Most of the other students mercifully disappeared, leaving Rachel to grieve in private. Only one teenager remained, gazing silently at Rachel, his face a mirror of her grief and shame. Rachel felt his presence hovering nearby her and raised her head to see who it was. Their eyes meet with a flash of recognition and a jolt of intrigue. Rachel remembered the boy in front of her, his face glimpsed in passing once or twice before, but the sense of familiarity ran much deeper than that casual recognition would imply. He pushed a rebellious lock of brown hair out of his bright blue eyes as he stared at her.

Cameron's heart beat erratically in his chest as his eyes locked on Rachel's. He knew this must be the girl from the accident. He recognized the golden hair he had glimpsed from across the hospital room. Lank and matted against her pillow, it had still been lovely to look at, but now it glistened like honey as it fell in gentle waves beside her face. Tubes and wires had blocked his view of her graceful features, disguising her beauty with the medical paraphernalia requisite to her survival. But now, even twisted in anguish, her tender face was beautiful to him as he gazed upon it for the first time. Why did she seem so familiar to him? He wondered as he gaped at her, eyes wide and mouth open. Her perplexity was just as evident as his.

"I'm Cameron," he offered quietly, slowly approaching the teary-eyed girl.

"I'm so sorry!" they blurted, their voices in unison as Rachel jumped up to meet him, remorse etched deeply into her face. Their expressions cycled from regret to surprise as they realized they bore the same sense of blame.

"It's not your fault, Rachel. How could it possibly be your fault?" Cameron 's hands impulsively reached to caress her cheek. Rachel's eyes widened at his touch but she didn't flinch.

"He was taking me home. I didn't want my mom to come get me. I didn't want her to see where I was, what we were doing." Rachel's hazel eyes locked onto his as she made her confession. "He was too drunk to drive, I should have seen that, but I let him drive anyway..." she dropped her gaze at this admission, and a tear welled up and dripped onto Cameron's wrist.

Though he didn't remember it, Cameron had heard the story about the accident. He knew Jason had been intoxicated, Rachel too. The police had cleared him of any fault in the situation — Rachel's statement to the police had helped, but he still wondered what really happened that night. Had his own behavior been just as much to blame? Surely he could have avoided the accident if he'd been more alert. His loss of memory served as his punishment, but Jason's fate was so much worse.

"I'm so sorry you lost your memory, Cameron. I can't imagine what you're going through. I would give anything to go back and change what happened that night." Her eyes pleaded silently for forgiveness.

"I don't blame you, Rachel, not at all. And I'm sorry you lost your boyfriend. I wish I could go back and do it all over again, too. They tell me I was driving home from the convenience store — just had to have some Mountain Dew and Cheetos. Seriously? Why couldn't I be satisfied with whatever was in the fridge? That just sounds disgusting anyway!" A small smile escaped Cameron's grimace, and Rachel felt a tiny ray of light break through her despair.

"Snack choices aren't usually considered a life-altering decision," Rachel said, a hint of jest lightening her own solemnity. They didn't know what else to say to each other, but the tardy bell interrupted their stilted attempts at humor, and the pair offered each other fumbled goodbyes as they hastily departed for their classrooms, both turning back for one last glance as they walked away.

Rachel realized that Tara must have slipped away sometime during her strange encounter with Cameron. She wondered how much of their exchange she had witnessed and if it had appeared as odd to her as it had felt to Rachel. As uncomfortable as it had been, Rachel found herself regretting the end of the conversation, and she hoped briefly that their paths might cross again.

Sneaking quietly into first period, her eyes met Kelsey's, and Rachel recoiled at her venomous stare. Clearly not everyone had absolved Rachel of her guilt. The entire class stared at her as she fumbled into the only open seat, some with curiosity, others with disdain. No one spoke to her except the teacher who called her up after class. He mumbled some meaningless condolences before asking to collect her work.

Second period offered more curious stares and uncomfortable silences, and Rachel felt like it was her first day all over again. She was relieved to see Tara's friendly face waiting for her in literature. Mercifully, Tara didn't display the solemn, mournful look everyone else affected when they looked at Rachel, and she didn't feel the need to offer more sympathies. Instead, she whispered the latest gossip behind the teacher's back and made dramatic gestures to emphasize the high points of her stories. Rachel was incredibly grateful for the normality.

At lunch, Rachel happily rejoined the science club table, steering clear of Jason's crowd altogether. If Kelsey's reaction was any indication, they would't be too happy to see her anyway. Did they felt any guilt at all for their part in what happened, or did they blame it all on Jason or Rachel? Most likely the latter, knowing them.

Tara's friends, on the other hand, seemed thrilled to have her back. Reggie and Garrett both jumped up to greet her, Reggie engulfing her whole body in an overpowering bear hug and Garrett bobbing hyperactively before coming in for an awkward squeeze. "I got you a present, Rachel! I saw this in Hot Topic and knew you had to have it." Garrett handed Rachel a tee shirt that said, "Dain bramage. Suff ned."

"Thanks, Garret. That's awesome," Rachel replied genuinely. She needed a new night shirt.

Eve offered a cheerful smile and wave, and Tyler bowed like a gentleman to Rachel and Tara before pulling out a chair for his girlfriend. Rachel was pleased to see her match-making skills were still successful. Everyone offered the obligatory greetings and sympathies, but they didn't dwell on the tragedy, and the conversation soon shifted to something tech-y and complicated that went right over Rachel's head. Her attention drifted to the scene around her until her eyes landed on Cameron, exiting the lunch line.

His sights focused on the lunch table in front of him, presumably where he usually sat, but most of the students there paid him no mind and the ones that did looked less than thrilled to see him. His steps wavered as he caught their uninviting glances, and he stopped halfway to the table. Rachel watched as his eyes roamed the rest of the cafeteria, looking for a friendlier reaction, but everyone else seemed caught up in their own little world, oblivious to the needs of others.

Without a second thought, when Cameron's gaze passed by her Rachel offered a cautious wave, nodding towards the empty seat beside her. Cameron blinked in surprise, his head doing a double take as he halted his perusal and turned back towards Rachel. Skeptical, his expression silently questioned her invitation, and she answered with a grin and a nod. The conversation faltered as Cameron approached the table, and curious eyes jumped back and forth between him and Rachel.

"Hey, guys, this is Cameron." Rachel pulled out the empty chair next to her. Their stares were full of unanswered questions, but Rachel didn't elaborate, and they quickly recovered their composure and offered friendly greetings to the newcomer. Rachel smiled in satisfaction. She knew her friends would be cool with it. Cameron offered a grateful smile to Rachel as he settled in beside her.

"Old friends not exactly rolling out the Welcome Wagon, huh?" Rachel asked.

"Uh, no," Cameron replied, disheartened. "I don't know what the old me was like, but apparently he was a lot cooler than the new me. It's not like I can help it that I don't get their inside jokes or can't remember that trip we took to the lake last year or why I shouldn't mention underwear when Allison is around."

The rest of the table tittered as Rachel looked confused. "I don't get it either. Why shouldn't you mention underwear around Allison?"

"Well, I've since been told that Allison didn't wear underwear to school one day and her skirt got caught up in her waistband when she went to the bathroom. I guess she walked around for quite awhile with her 'assets' on display before somebody finally told her," Cameron explained with a chuckle. "I obviously didn't remember that, and I got reamed by the whole table when I casually asked the girls how many of them ever worried about panty lines."

"Why the heck did you ask that?!" Rachel sputtered, narrowly avoiding shooting milk out her nose. The rest of the table was cracking up.

"Well, I overheard my mom going on and on the other day about my sister's visible panty lines and I thought it was funny, so I..." Cameron faltered as he realized everyone was staring skeptically at him, barely holding their laughter.

"I was just trying to make conversation," Cameron shrugged pathetically. The giggles turned to guffaws as he hung his head in mock humiliation.

"I can't imagine why they don't like you, Cameron," Rachel teased with sincerity. "I think you're pretty funny."

When the bell rang, Cameron followed Rachel into her algebra classroom. "I know we're friends and all now, but shouldn't you be going to your own class now?"

"This IS my class." Cameron gave her a curious look.

"Really? I don't remember you being in here before. Weird." Come to think of it, she couldn't really remember seeing half the kids in the room. Maybe it was because she only had eyes for Jason before. She ignored Kelsey and took an open seat near Cameron, which turned out to be a really good, or really bad, idea. Every time Mr. Volnar turned around, Cameron whispered another joke in Rachel's ear. The wisecracks left Rachel holding her stomach, trying not to laugh, until it dawned on her that Rider had done the same thing their first day here, and her laughter ebbed as sorrow enveloped her.

Cameron could see her delight dissolve into sadness, but he didn't question it. He understood how the pain crept up on you at the oddest moments, how the littlest things could make you remember all you had lost. Making Rachel laugh felt right, though, almost familiar. Being with her was like being with an old friend, even though he knew they weren't friends before. He certainly didn't feel that way about any of his so-called old friends. They were all strangers to him now, and they way they acted didn't make him want to revive those relationships. The only person he really had any desire to be with was Rachel, and yet he had only known her for a few hours. How weird was that? He decided he didn't care.

"Hey Rachel," Cameron whispered suddenly when the teacher was busy writing an equation on the board, "you wanna, uh, hang out, or uh, something after school?" Real smooth, he thought, abashedly. Shoulda thought that one through a little more. He could see the wheels turning as she contemplated his offer, not sure if he was interested in friendship or something more. He wasn't really sure about that himself.

"It's just, my old friends don't really understand me anymore and, I don't know, it seems like you do," he quickly explained before she had a chance to turn him down.

Rachel's expression softened and he knew she sympathized with his feelings. "Sure, Cameron, that would be fun," she replied kindly.

"My place or yours?" Cameron dared a saucy wink.

"Uh, I think we better make it my house for my parents' sake. They're still pretty worked up about the fact that I had a boyfriend they didn't know about. And I'm not sure they'll ever let me go to anybody else's house ever again after they found out about what was going on at that party," Rachel explained guiltily.

"Yeah, I heard about that. Do you party like that a lot?"

"God, no!" Rachel exclaimed, a little too loudly. Mr. Volnar gave her a noxious look but didn't say anything. Apparently her status as tragedy victim bought her a little grace from her teachers. The other students gawked disbelievingly as he returned to his lecture without a reprimand.

When she was sure he was absorbed in his calculations, Rachel expounded on her denial. "I'd never done any of that before! But I think Jason's friends did it all the time. At least that's the way it seemed that night. It was stupid of me to even try it, but I just wanted to fit in. They were having such a good time and I thought, what could it hurt to try, just this once? I was... an idiot. But Jason made me feel special, and his friends were like, the coolest kids in this school. I didn't want to look like a loser in front of them. I should have just had him take me home right away, then none of this would've happened." Rachel face dropped as guilt overwhelmed her.

"You can't think that way, Rachel," Cameron laid a tentative hand on hers. "It's terrible that Jason died, but he made his own choices. You can't shoulder the blame for all of it."

"But what about you, Cameron? How can you even stand to be around me, knowing that, if it wasn't for me, you wouldn't be where you are now?" Her heart expected rejection, but her eyes held out hope for reprieve.

"If none of this had happened, I might never have gotten to know you, Rachel, and you seem like a pretty cool person to know," Cameron offered with a gentle smile. Rachel just shook her head in disbelief. "Look, I don't remember what my life was like before, so I don't even know what I'm missing. It's really not all that terrible, just... disconcerting. But I'm not going to let that ruin the rest of my life. Maybe someday I'll remember it, maybe I won't, but for right now I just want to do what makes me feel happy. And hanging out with you after school sounds fun." Cameron gave a playful shrug and Rachel couldn't help but smile. Cameron was a pretty amazing guy, and being with him almost made the pain go away.

Soulmate

As the rest of the afternoon dragged, Rachel found herself thinking more and more about Cameron. She didn't understand why she felt so drawn to someone she had just met. She even felt a little guilty about it, like she didn't have enough guilt already. She just lost her boyfriend and already she was attracted to some other guy? The feelings were different from the ones she had for Jason, though. She couldn't explain it, but she felt connected to Cameron, like old friends or something.

Reggie distracted her during art class with talk of a party coming up soon. Since all of the science-clubbers had birthdays around the same time, they threw one big party for all of them the third weekend in April. Reggie was blown away to learn that Rachel's birthday just happened to be that same day.

"NO WAY! Ain't NO way!" Reggie bellowed when Rachel insisted she was born on April 18th. "Well, you just gonna be the star of this year's party then, ain't ya?"

"So how does this party work, Reggie? Can I, like, invite people?" Her first thoughts were of Paige, but she couldn't help but think of Cameron a little bit, too.

"Sure! Invite as many as you like, girl! The party's gonna be at Tara's place, and her house be like... huge, you know? Everybody just brings somethin'."

Just then, Rachel remembered again that she might have a hard time getting approval from her parents to go to another party. "What if I had it at my house instead?" She blurted. "I mean, you guys have probably all hosted it before, right? So it would be only fair for me to take a turn. Unless you think Tara would mind."

"Naw, girl. She don't care. She'd probably be happy 'bout it. Party plannin' ain't her thing. Hey... I ain't never been to your pad. Is it sweet?" Reggie's eyebrows wiggling dramatically.

"Sure, if you're into Craftsman style furniture and Precious Moments figurines," Rachel teased, excited about the idea. She'd never had a big birthday party before; it was usually just her and Paige. She hoped her parents would be okay with it, but they were so thrilled that she was alive and well that they would probably give her just about anything she wanted.

She was still daydreaming about the party when Cameron met her at her locker after school. She wanted to tell him all about it, but she decided she better get permission from her parents before she started inviting people.

"Hey Rach," Cameron greeted as he approached her locker. With his head down and his shoulders hunched, his body language indicated self doubt. Didn't he realize how handsome he was? With his dark brown hair swooping over bright blue eyes and his athletic physique, surely he had no trouble attracting girls before. Of course, he wouldn't remember that. As far as he knew, everyone thought he was a freak. That realization actually made her feel a little better about spending time with him when she was still mourning Jason. It was almost like a public service, really. Yeah, right.

"Hey Cam, let me just pack my books and I'll be

ready to go. I don't know about you, but I have a ton of homework. It's like they're trying to make up for the whole week of spring break on the first day back." Rachel rolled her eyes dramatically as she shoved her textbooks into her backpack.

"Yeah, I have a lot, too. Maybe we can do our algebra homework together?" Cameron suggested, holding her backpack for her so she could force the last book inside.

"Sure, that sounds good. Wait, how are we getting to my house? Do you have another car already? I always take the bus. I'm not old enough to get my license yet," Rachel rambled nervously.

"Yeah, with the insurance I was able to get a new car. Well, new to me anyway. My parents picked out the safest vehicle they could find. The ugliest one too, I think," Cameron explained as they made their way to the parking lot. Sure enough, the monstrosity Cameron led her to looked like a tank. He opened the door for her and tossed her bag into the back before helping her up into the high seat.

"Does it scare you to drive again?" Rachel asked when Cameron nervously adjusted his seat and mirrors and took a big breath before starting the engine.

"A little," Cameron admitted. "What's weird is, I feel like I don't really know what I'm doing, you know? I mean, I feel like I've never driven before. I guess it's just the memory loss. Maybe I should take Driver's Ed again." Rachel chuckled but Cameron could sense her hesitation. "Are you sure you want to ride with me?" he asked seriously.

"Yeah, yeah, it's fine. I trust you," Rachel assured him, forcing a smile.

When they got to her house, Rachel led Cameron to the kitchen to scrounge up a snack. Finding the Mountain Dew her father always kept in the fridge, Rachel was amused to also discover a bag of Cheetos in the pantry.

"Ta da!" She exclaimed, holding out the treats to Cameron.

"Hmm, those are regular, I prefer jalapeño cheddar. Maybe we should run to the store," Cameron responded seriously, but his face gave him away before Rachel could compose a response. Her expression switched from stunned to surprised as she realized he was joking.

"How could you?" She wailed, feigning offense.

"More like, how could you fall for that?" Cameron teased, plucking the Cheetos from her hand and shoving some into his mouth.

Rachel gave him a playful smack and nodded towards the stairs. "Let's go to my room."

Rachel's bedroom wasn't quite as embarrassing as the one in her old home. That one had bubble gum pink walls dotted with peeling stickers and pictures of cute celebrities torn from the pages of Teen Beat magazine. She still had the girly, white painted furniture of her childhood bedroom, but her bed was dressed in the new, more grown-up teal silk comforter her mom had bought for her when they moved. Nervous about going back to school, she had woken up early that morning and had even made the bed, taking the time to straighten the wrinkles out of the covers and fluff the piles of decorative pillows. The curtains matched the bedding, so the room looked pretty good even though the walls and carpet were still standard builder's beige.

Get well cards lined the top of her dresser and window ledge, and a deflated bouquet of helium balloons dragged lazily along the floor, its tail of curled ribbon fluttering in the airflow from the heating vent. She was glad she had finally thrown out the welcome home flowers that had sat wilting next to her bed till all the petals fell off and the water in the vase turned a murky brown. A framed picture of Paige and Rachel from last year sat on her night stand, and Cameron picked it up and studied their faces.

"This is your friend from the hospital. Paige, right?"

"Yeah, we've been friends forever." Rachel's eyes softened at the memories. "I couldn't imagine life without her, but look at me now — a whole new group of friends. I still miss her like crazy, though." Her thoughts drifted to Rider, who she missed even more, and her face turned solemn.

"I'm really sorry you lost him. Were you in love?" Cameron asked, sensing the pain he saw on her face was about more than just being away from her friend.

"No, it wasn't like that. Maybe it could've been, if things were different. I mean, I loved him with all my heart, but... wait, are you talking about Jason?" Rachel shook her head in confusion and surprise. What was she doing, talking about Rider like that? She was usually so careful.

"Yeaahhhh,... who are you talking about?" Cameron asked, curiously.

Rachel shook her head empathically. "Nothing, nobody."

"So you lost somebody else, too. That's rough," Cameron empathized, taking a seat on the edge of her bed. "Do you want to talk about it?"

Rachel plopped down next to him with a sigh. "No, I can't... you wouldn't... I mean, it's... complicated." She sighed.

"I'm a pretty good listener, I think, and I promise not to judge," Cameron offered with a smile.

Rachel desperately wished she could talk about it, wished there was someone else who could understand, but no one ever had except for Paige. Everyone else had thought she was crazy. So why was she so tempted to share her deepest secret with this boy she barely knew?

"So there was a boy, who you loved, but you weren't in love, but maybe you could've been, and somehow you lost him..." Cameron prodded, nudging her playfully with his shoulder.

"You wouldn't understand, Cameron. It's just, not something I talk about, okay?" Rachel mumbled, forcing herself not to look into his eyes. She knew if she did she would tell him everything, and then he would run.

"It's okay, Rachel. You don't have to tell me all your secrets — yet," Cameron teased, wiggling his eyebrows. "Let's do our homework so we can be done in time to watch *The Batchelor*."

Rachel's eyes bugged out and she erupted in laughter. "You watch *The Batchelor*?"

Cameron stumbled over his words, trying to salvage his masculinity. "Well, you know, there's a lot of sexy women on there!"

"Oh my God, Cameron, you are too much! Do you want to borrow my copy of Cosmo?"

Cameron's face reddened, but he managed to retort, "I've heard there are some really good articles in there, so yeah maybe!"

* * * * * * *

A few hours later, Cameron and Rachel were diligently studying when Mrs. Masterson got home. "How was your first day back, sweetheart?" Mary asked, poking her head into Rachel's room. Her eyes widened when she saw Cameron lounging next to Rachel on the bed.

"Oh, hey Mom." Rachel popped up and rushed to whisper in her mother's ear. "This is Cameron, from school. We're just studying together. Would it be okay if he stayed for dinner?"

"Uh, sure honey," Mary faltered, "Cameron?" she whispered back, "Like, as in, the Cameron from the accident?"

"Yeah, Mom, he's... cool." Rachel's facial expression begged her mom not to make a scene.

"It's nice to meet you, Cameron," Mary recovered. Cameron had extricated himself from the pile of pillows on Rachel's bed and approached Mrs. Masterson with a polite smile, hand extended in greeting.

"Nice to meet you, too, Mrs. Masterson."

"Well, how well-mannered you are!" Mary put a hand to her chest and cooed. "You're welcome to stay the evening, Cameron. Dinner will be ready in an hour."

"Thank you, ma'am." Cameron nodded. "Would you like us to help you?"

Mary's mouth fell open in surprise. "Well, that is very kind of you to offer! But it looks like you two have enough work to keep you busy for a while longer." Mary glanced at the huge pile of books spilling from their bags.

"Tons," Rachel confirmed with an emphatic nod.

"I'll just call you when it's ready then." Mary hesitated, debating for a moment, then finally left, leaving the door open halfway.

Rachel's father was similarly impressed by Cameron when he got home just in time for dinner, so Rachel decided it was a good time to ask about the party she wanted to have for her birthday. She figured her parents would be less likely to freak out about it in front of a guest.

"So, these friends I have at school, the science club kids," Rachel didn't want to confuse them with Jason's group of friends, "they have this tradition every April where they throw one big birthday party for all of them."

"Well, that's interesting," Mary replied cautiously, blowing on a spoonful of chili.

"Yeah and, since my birthday is this month, they thought they'd celebrate my birthday then, too." Rachel's parents were quiet, not willing to commit till they heard all the details. "So, I thought, maybe we should have the party here," Rachel explained. Rob and Mary exchanged dubious glances but didn't outright deny her, so Rachel continued. "It wouldn't have to be any trouble, really. Everybody would bring something. And I would clean it all up afterwards," Rachel promised.

More thoughtful looks passed between her parents before her father finally spoke. "It's okay with me if your mother doesn't mind. I'd rather have you stay home anyway."

Rachel's mother gave a quick nod, and a huge smile took over Rachel's face. She was hoping that would help her case. She turned to Cameron excitedly and asked, "So, Cameron, wanna come to my birthday party this Saturday?!"

Cameron chuckled. "Wouldn't miss it."

Later, the two teenagers sat on the couch in the living room, chatting like sports commentators on the different qualities displayed by each of the beautiful women vying for the bachelor's heart. Rachel was surprised to realize that she was the one sizing up their body parts while Cameron was focused more on their personalities, just like when she and Rider had watched the show. In fact, everything about the evening reminded her of being with Rider. She and Cameron had an easy camaraderie that felt completely natural, like they had known each other for years instead of just hours. Cameron, too, felt so comfortable that he practically forgot he didn't live there. Only after a few odd looks from Rachel's parents did he realize it was late and he should probably go home.

"Thanks for coming over today, Cameron, I had a really good time," Rachel said as she walked him to the door.

"Me, too, Rach, you're the nicest person I've met in a really long time." His gaze traveled from her eyes to her lips and he realized he desperately wanted to kiss her. He settled instead for running a hand down her golden hair. "You have really beautiful hair, you know that? I remember looking at it when I was in the hospital, how this one lock of it always dangled off the bed." Rachel blushed as her eyes dropped to her feet. "Goodnight Rachel. I'll see you tomorrow," he said, as he headed towards his car, without taking his eyes off her. It came out like a promise.

Rachel drifted happily up to her room, all her troubles forgotten as she basked in the warmth of Cameron's attention. "Good night, Rider, wherever you are," she whispered as she climbed into bed. "I wish you could meet Cameron. I think you would really like him." She fell asleep dreaming of Cameron and Rider together, hanging out like pals.

* * * * * * *

Cameron drove slowly and carefully back to his own home after finally leaving Rachel's house. His mind was awhirl with all that had happened that day. The day had started out like most others since his return to school, with apathy and dread. His brother had been bugging him to throw the ball around with him after school like they used to, his sister was upset because he had teased her about having freckles which was apparently a big no-no in his house, and his mother had packed him "his favorite lunch" which turned out to be tuna fish salad and some gluten-free crackers — disgusting tree-hugger food in his opinion, which he had quickly disposed of as soon as he left the house that morning. He kind of understood now why he had felt the need to make a munchie run so late in the evening the night of the accident. The only snack food his mother kept in the house was veggie chips and Larabars.

He took his time getting back to his house. He hated to admit it, but he just didn't feel any emotional connection to his family at all. They were nice enough, but he just didn't seem to belong with them. He felt more comfortable after five minutes with Rachel's family than he did after five weeks of trying to fit in with his own. Maybe if they accepted him for who he was now it would be different, but they kept trying to turn him back into the old Cameron, and the mold just didn't seem to fit anymore.

When he got to his house, he noticed most of the windows were dark, so he snuck quietly in through the back door, trying not to wake his family. He barely made it past the mudroom before he was met by the fiercely blazing glare of his mother. She was seated at the kitchen table with a magazine and a cup of tea, arms folded in consternation as she stared him down like a hunter about to attack her prey. She looked ferocious despite the fuzzy pink bathrobe and slippers.

"Where on God's green earth have you been all night, young man?" she demanded with a scowl. Cameron opened his mouth to answer but she wasn't done with her tirade. "Do you have any idea how worried I've been about you? It is 11pm and you are just coming home from school? Well? Answer me, Cameron! Where have you been all day?!"

Cameron was quick to apologize for fear that his mother was about to implode. "I'm sorry, Mom! I didn't think. I went to a friend's house after school to hang out. I should have told you. I'm sorry!"

"You're darn right, you should have told me! How was I supposed to know where you were? I've been worried sick all day that something had happened to you again!"

"Why didn't you just call me?" Cameron asked.

His question was sincere, but his mother obviously didn't see it that way.

"Don't you dare get smart with me, young man!" she roared, her face a terrifying caricature of her normally angelic demeanor. "What do you think I've been doing all evening? I called your cell phone dozens of times before your father discovered it buried under a pile of papers on your desk. Then I called every one I knew and nobody had any idea where you were!"

"Oh, yeah, I guess I forgot my phone this morning," Cameron muttered, guiltily. He could never seem to remember to take that thing with him.

"In this house, we expect to know where you are when you're not home, do you understand me?"

"Yes, ma'am," Cameron agreed. "It won't happen again, I promise."

Mrs. Wilson was momentarily soothed by Cameron's acquiesce, but her anger was not completely appeased. "Now I want to know who this friend is that you've been with all day, because I spoke to every single person on your contact list, and you weren't with any of them!"

"I was with Rachel, Mom, the girl from the accident. She came back to school today and we met. We had a lot to talk about, you know?" Cameron rubbed a hand through his hair, mussing it.

Janice Wilson's anger faltered, and her expression

softened as she considered what her son had said. "You talked to her? How is she? Is she doing better?" The mother in her couldn't help but worry about the girl whose life had almost been lost.

"Yeah, Mom. She's doing great. I mean, considering. She was really nice to me, friendlier than most of my old friends have been. We just kind of hit it off, you know? So we decided to hang out after school. I honestly didn't even think about calling you to let you know, and I'm sorry for that. I totally should have. It was wrong of me to make you worry like that." Cameron's boyish charm shined through and melted his mother's anger completely.

"Oh Cameron, you are such a different person than you used to be. So much kinder and more respectful. I guess I can forgive a little forgetfulness." Janice reached out to hug her son. "Why don't you invite Rachel over here next time, okay? I'd like to get to know her a little bit, too, maybe make her a special dinner sometime."

Considering his mother's health food obsession, Cameron wasn't sure one of her homemade dinners would actually be a treat for Rachel, but he was happy to have an excuse to spend more time with her, so he eagerly agreed to extend his mother's invitation to Rachel the next time he saw her.

Cameron bid his mother goodnight then slowly climbed the stairs to his bedroom. He was mentally exhausted from all that had happened in one short day, but thrilled at the prospect of seeing Rachel again tomorrow.

Soulmate

For the first time since the accident, he finally had something to look forward to, some reason to be grateful he was still alive.

Chapter Eighteen

Coming back to school the second day after spring break was a lot less stressful than the first day had been, and it reminded Rachel of how she'd felt when she first came to Indy High, shy but anxious to reinvent herself.

Today she was anxious for a whole other reason -- the chance to see Cameron again. Not that her science club friends weren't great; they were fun to be with, and they made her feel welcome even though she didn't really fit in with them. But with Cameron, she felt like she'd finally found the friendship she'd been missing since she moved away from Paige.

She threw on some clothes, not really caring what she looked like, then laughed at herself, remembering how worried she'd been about her appearance when she was trying to impress Jason. Not that she didn't care what Cameron thought about her, but for some reason she felt like he accepted her for who she was, no matter what she wore or how she did her hair or makeup. He'd already seen her at her absolute worst, after all -- battered, head shaved, and comatose.

"You look a lot happier than yesterday," Tara said as Rachel slid in next to her on the bus. "First day back didn't turn out as bad as you thought it would?"

"Nope. Worse!" Rachel teased, knocking her elbow into Tara's.

"That was really nice of you to invite Cameron to sit with us yesterday. He looked like a little lost puppy dog."

"Yeah, he's had it pretty rough. He's cool, though. I like him."

Tara's eyes bugged out at Rachel's coy smile. "Oh my gosh, you *like him*-like him, don't you?!"

Rachel's face turned red, and she shrugged her shoulders but dropped her eyes, suddenly intent on her backpack. "Just as friends. I mean, it's too early to fall for another guy… isn't it?"

Rachel wondered what Tara would think if she knew the feelings she had already been having towards Cameron. She'd think she was a hussy for sure.

"Not really. I mean, Cameron seems like a really great guy; I can see the appeal. Besides, you and Jason hadn't been going out for that long when the accident happened. I think the connection just feels stronger because you shared such a traumatic experience. To be honest, I think if Jason hadn't died, the relationship wouldn't have lasted much longer anyway."

Rachel rolled her eyes. "Yeah, I know, you thought Jason just wanted to get into my pants and he would've dumped me once he did."

Tara cringed at her. "No! I mean, well yeah, that's what he usually did. But I think you would've figured out that he was a player before you let him get that far, and you would've dumped him. You're too smart to let some guy take advantage of you."

The compliment put the smile back on Rachel's face, and she tossed her hair, lifting her chin. "So what have you been up to since I've been gone anyway?"

Tara's face lit up as she started talking about her ideas for the next science fair, and Rachel tried to pay attention, but when Tara started using words that Rachel couldn't even pronounce, let alone understand, Rachel's mind drifted to other things, and her eyes glazed over as she nodded randomly, trying to appear interested.

Her eyes snapped back into focus, though, when the bus pulled up to the front of the school and she caught a glimpse of Cameron, leaning against the side of the building, looking amazing.

"What'd I say?" Tara asked, noticing Rachel's sudden perkiness. Her eyes followed Rachel's gaze, and she nodded her head with a smirk. "Go on, go talk to him. Looks like he's waiting for you, anyway."

Rachel gave a grateful smile and dashed off the bus. She forced herself to slow down as she got a little closer, not wanting to look too eager to see him, but his eyes followed her as she made her way towards him, and his face broke into a wide smile.

"Hey Cameron, whatcha doing?" She tried to sound casual, but her heart was thumping so loudly she was afraid he could hear it as it pounded for release.

Cameron shrugged and pulled himself away from the wall, trying to act nonchalant as well, but the gemstone sparkle in his eyes gave him away.

"Just wanted to tell you thanks for hanging out with me yesterday. It felt good not to be treated like a freak for a while." He shoved his hands in his pockets and dipped his head, hiding his embarrassed smile.

"I know the feeling," Rachel said, nudging into him with her elbow. "Would you like to sit with me at lunch again?"

Please say yes, please say yes! She silently begged him with her eyes, and Cameron rewarded her offer with a flashlight-bright smile.

"That sounds great — thanks. Your friends seem pretty cool. And you're not so bad, either," he teased, nudging her back.

They headed towards Rachel's locker, spending just a moment of silence in front of Jason's memorial on the way. "Was he a good boyfriend?" Cameron asked, and Rachel was taken aback by the question. He didn't ask, "Did you love him?" or "Do you miss him?" Those questions were hard enough, but instead, his question seemed more personal, more real, and dug deeper into the heart of

Rachel's wound than she was prepared for.

She hadn't known Jason long enough to really love him, and to be honest, she didn't really miss him. She missed how he made her feel about herself, but Tara was probably right. Jason wasn't that great of a boyfriend, or even a person, probably, but it still felt wrong to fault the dead.

"We hadn't been going out for that long." She said after a few moments of contemplation. The answer was kind of a cop out, but Cameron didn't question it, and somehow Rachel thought maybe he understood.

"So what can I do to help you get ready for the party?" Cameron asked as they neared her locker, trying to lighten the mood.

"I don't know; I've never had a big party before. What do you think we should do?"

The spent the remaining few minutes discussing party plans, their heads bent together over Rachel's cell phone as they searched online for ideas. When the bell rang, Rachel lifted her head to say goodbye, and she caught herself about to lean in for a kiss. She pulled away quickly, realizing her faux pas, and tried to cover the awkwardness with chatter, but she caught the look on Cameron's face when he realized what she was about to do, and she would swear she saw desire there. Was it possible that Cameron liked her that way, too?

They ate lunch at the science club table again, and Cameron joked that his messed up brain should be the focus of their upcoming science fair project. Once he had broached the subject, the others were all curious about his strange experience, and they peppered him with questions.

"I feel like my past was all a dream, and I'm just now waking up for the first time," Cameron said, trying to explain it. "Everything feels new to me, like I've never done it before, yet, it all feels familiar at the same time."

This led to a lively discussion about neural pathways that left Rachel and Cameron's eyes glazed over. They glanced at each other and burst into simultaneous laughter, noticing the same spaced-out look in each other's eyes.

In Algebra class, they sat together in the back of the room, and Rachel noticed Kelsey giving her the stink eye when she started whispering to Cameron, but Rachel ignored her, no longer desirous of her approval.

The new math concept seemed a little challenging to Rachel, so she tried to pay more attention to Mr. Volnar, even though all she really wanted to do was make fun of him behind his back to Cameron.

"I'm not sure I get this new stuff," Cameron admitted as they left the classroom, rubbing a hand through his hair. "Do you wanna work on the homework together? We could hang out at my place if you'd like."

Rachel's mood instantly lifted like a balloon filled with helium, and she smiled and nodded. "Sounds great. I'm not sure my parents are ready for me to be out of their sight yet, though, so do you think you could come over to my place instead?"

Cameron agreed eagerly. He really felt more comfortable at her house, anyway. Plus, with no siblings around, they'd have a little more privacy. He wasn't sure why they needed it — it wasn't like they were gonna make out or anything, but for some reason, he felt the most comfortable when he and Rachel were alone.

After school, Cameron met Rachel by her locker again, and they headed towards her house. They plopped on the bed with the half-eaten bag of Cheetos and dug into their algebra homework, but Cameron couldn't concentrate.

He was distracted by the smell of Rachel's citrus-scented shampoo and the way he caught a whiff of it every time she moved her hair. One errant lock kept falling in front of her face, and she would flip it behind her shoulder, only to have it fall again whenever she twisted her head. He loved when she turned her eyes towards him, and he loved that little tease of citrus. He wanted to bury his nose in her long, blonde locks and take a deep whiff, but instead he satisfied himself by constantly asking her questions so she would turn and look at him.

When she did, their faces would be so close, he could feel her breath on his cheek, and it made him wonder what she tasted like. His gaze would drop from her eyes to her lips   , and he wondered what she would do if he reached out and kissed her. He had no experience whatsoever with kissing, at least not that he remembered, but the way she smiled at him with those plump lips made him want to own them. Would she reciprocate if he kissed her, or would she be upset with him? He thought she might be interested, the way her own eyes drifted down towards his lips occasionally, but he wasn't completely sure, and he was too chicken to risk it.

Of course, when she looked at him like that it made him feel woozy inside, and eventually he flopped over onto his back and stared at the ceiling, needing a reprieve from the intensity.

"Aren't girls' rooms usually plastered in movie star posters or something?" he asked, letting his eyes wander around the blank walls of her bedroom.

Rachel laughed and turned over onto her back beside him. "Yeah, I guess so. Mine used to be, back in Michigan. We only lived here for a few weeks before the accident, so I didn't get a chance to do much decorating."

"Let me guess, you had posters of... Louis Tomlinson?" Cameron had a picture in his mind of Rachel lying under a poster of the oldest One Direction band member, and the image was so vivid he would've sworn it was a memory.

Rachel gasped and swatted him on the arm. "How'd you know that?"

Cameron grinned. "Lucky guess, I suppose."

Rachel scrunched her nose as she stared intently at him. "You know, you kinda look like Louis Tomlinson."

"Is that a good thing?"

Rachel shrugged but gave a coy smile. "Most girls think he's pretty cute."

He opened his mouth to ask her if she thought he

was cute, but then dropped an arm over his face instead. He was too embarrassed. Instead, he settled for, "Is that your type?"

Rachel snorted. "What? Pop stars? Yeah, totally." Her lips twisted in a grin then grew more serious. "I don't think I really have a type. I've only been on two dates in my life, and the second one ended in tragedy." Her lips puckered as she held in a tear.

"Don't take this the wrong way, but from what I've heard, Jason didn't always make the best choices."

Rachel shook her head and cringed. "No, he wasn't exactly the best boyfriend material."

Cameron turned to look her in the eye, curious to understand her better. "So why were you going out with him?"

Rachel sighed and drew lazy circles on her belly as she contemplated the answer to that. She was embarrassed by the truth, but for some reason she felt compelled to tell it. Her eyes begged him for understanding as she met his gaze. "Jason made me feel... special, and no one else ever had."

"I think you're special, Rachel," Cameron whispered, daring to stroke a finger down her cheek.

Chapter Nineteen

The day of Rachel's birthday party bloomed bright and full of promise as Rachel woke up with a smile on her face and a skip in her step. Her mother had gotten excited about the idea of a big party and had gone all out for it, purchasing balloons and streamers and ordering platters of Chick-fil-A nuggets and a gigantic birthday cake. Rachel could hear her thumping around downstairs, presumably cleaning every square inch of the house, even though Rachel had agreed to do it herself.

It had been a pretty great week already. Her science club friends had happily accepted Cameron into the fold and made him and Rachel feel like lifetime members of the group. They had spent a lot of the week talking about the party, so Rachel didn't feel as left out of the conversation as she did when they were off on one of their more scientific tangents. Cameron had become the doll of the club, his quick wit and gregarious nature made him a perfect foil for their sometimes overly serious intellectual discussions.

Rachel and Cameron had spent almost every afternoon together, doing homework, watching TV, and talking and talking about everything under the sun. Rachel's parents had warmed up to Cameron so quickly that they happily allowed her to go to his house as well. It probably helped that Cameron assured them his parents and siblings would be there too.

At his house, Cameron showed her his baseball card collection, which apparently had been pretty important to pre-accident Cameron, because it was lovingly sorted by year and team into highly protective display albums. Post-accident Cameron didn't recognize any of the players, but he found himself flipping through the albums occasionally, trying to stir up some of his old passion. Baseball players just didn't excite him, though. Neither did playing baseball, or watching baseball, or listening to his dad talk endlessly about baseball. The only thing that stirred any passion in Cameron now was the thought of being with Rachel.

Being with her felt like coming home where he finally belonged, but it was new and exciting at the same time, too. Hanging out with her was like hanging out with his oldest pal, and although he couldn't remember any of his childhood friends, he imagined he had once had a buddy he could be himself around, somebody who understood him and loved him for who he was, because that's how Rachel made him feel, and it felt... comfortable, like a favorite pair of jeans. But Rachel sparked a whole other set of feelings in him too, a slow burn of passion that ignited to a full boil whenever she got too close. Every time he looked at her he wanted to kiss her and touch her, but he was afraid he might ruin the perfection of their friendship by initiating romance.

Although Cameron hadn't made any romantic moves towards Rachel yet, she could sense his attraction with every word and gaze. She supposed that his gentlemanly sense of propriety kept him from declaring his feelings so soon after she had lost her last love, but she knew he was falling for her and she for him. She figured she might have to make the first move, and she had decided she couldn't wait any longer.

Jason was just a distant memory now, it seemed. She loved the amazing way he had made her feel when he complimented her and kissed her and told her she was special, but she realized now that those were the only reasons she liked him. Cameron, on the other hand, was someone she could talk to, someone she had things in common with, and she felt almost the same rush of pleasure just being with him, without all the other romantic trappings.

She could only imagine how it would feel when he finally gave in and kissed her. It was going to happen tonight, she decided. One way or another. Either he was going to kiss her of his own accord, or she was going to kiss him. She knew she wouldn't be rebuffed.

She was also excited about Paige coming to visit. Her parents were heading down that morning so they would arrive in plenty of time for Paige to help Rachel pick out the perfect party outfit. On the only evening that week that Rachel hadn't spent with Cameron, she had instead spent hours on the phone with Paige talking about Cameron. Paige, having met Cameron just briefly at the hospital but enamored with him all the same, had been the one to persuade Rachel to make the first move herself.

"He's so much like Rider!" Rachel had told Paige while chatting the other day. "His jokes, his sarcastic comments, his willingness to watch chick flicks and cheesy sitcoms, even his compliments are just like the ones Rider used to give me." So much so, one time she had even called Cameron Rider and then had to fumble through an uncomfortable, half-truth explanation of who he was. Rachel figured Paige thought she was just imagining the similarities because she missed Rider so much, so she was anxious for Paige to get to know him better so she could see them for herself.

When Paige arrived, Rachel was stringing the last of the streamers in the dining room. Rachel's mom didn't know what colors to decorate with since the party was for everybody not just for Rachel, so she chose a rainbow theme and got streamers and balloons in just about every color available. Rachel worried that it looked a little bit like a gay pride parade, but Paige, who's bedroom was decorated similarly, assured her it was cute and creative, and Rachel figured her friends were cool enough to think it was campy and fun instead of weird or childish.

Cameron was the next to arrive, a bouquet of daisies in hand, and he came early under the premise of helping, but most of the work was already done, so he and Paige and Rachel all hovered around the buffet table, snatching bites of chicken and scoops of the chili cheese dip Cameron had brought — Rachel's favorite. Paige, being her typical gregarious self, decided to break the ice a little.

"So Cameron," Paige asked, an innocent look on her face but a devious gleam in her eye, "my friend Rachel here tells me she thinks you have the hots for her, but you haven't done anything about it yet. Is that so?"

Cameron choked on the bite of chicken in his mouth, and his face turned bright red, either from embarrassment or lack of oxygen or both, Rachel couldn't tell. "Paige!" Rachel scolded, halfheartedly, secretly glad that Paige had broached the subject.

"So? What gives, Coma Boy? Do you like her or not?"

Cameron was literally saved by the bell as the doorbell rang, and Rachel reluctantly went to answer it. She would have much preferred to hear Cameron's answer, though. She could hear Paige goading him in the background, but couldn't make out his reply. The party guests all arrived shortly thereafter so Rachel, too wrapped up in hostess duties, never got back to the conversation.

Rachel's friends were happy to meet Paige, who they had heard a lot about already, and Paige had a good time telling them embarrassing stories about Rachel's childhood while they all stood around munching on junk food. Cameron seemed incredibly fascinated by the stories, Paige noticed, so she really hammed it up, sparing Rachel no embarrassment. Cameron's favorite seemed to be the one about how Rachel used to treat her cat like a baby doll and dress it up in doll clothes when she played house. His face affected a peculiar, nostalgic gaze as he listened intently to Paige's ramblings. This led to similar revelations about all of the other party guests, each person trying their best to outdo the story told about them with a worse one about someone else.

The only person who didn't have anything to say was Cameron, and Rachel realized much too late that he had no stories to tell — about himself or anyone else. When she finally noticed his discomfort, Rachel decided to change the subject and popped up out of her seat to turn up the music.

The song on the stereo was "Shake It Off" and, inspired by the goofy dances Taylor Swift did in her music video, Rachel declared a "dance off" and dragged the others to their feet. Soon the kids were competing to see who could come up with the craziest dance moves, and Cameron looked a little more at ease. He was a terrible dancer, but he didn't seem to mind embarrassing himself. He bopped and boogied like a drunk uncle three hours into a wedding reception.

When the party-goers were too exhausted to dance another step, they all happily collapsed on the couches as Rachel's mom came out with a cake ablaze with candles and led them in a round of "Happy Birthday" that deteriorated into a fit of giggles when they reached the "Happy birthday, dear --" line, because everyone sang something different.

Mary attempted to make casual conversation as she served up gigantic slices of chocolate cake and scoops of vanilla ice cream by asking them each in turn when their actual birthdays were. Midway through the conversation, in atypical nerdiness Rachel pointed out that all the birthdates so far were multiples of three. "Mine is 18, so that fits too! What about yours, Cameron?" Rachel asked eagerly.

The conversation stalled as Cameron contemplated the question with a look of bewilderment, his fingers fumbling distractedly with the food on his plate. "Uh, May... something, maybe?" He croaked self-consciously, dropping his gaze. His first thought had been April 18th, but that couldn't be right. Surely his parents would've mentioned something if today was his birthday, too. His awkward answer left an uncomfortable silence since no one else knew when his birthday was either.

Mary broke the silence by suggesting they open presents, and the kids reanimated as Rachel passed out the gifts Santa-style. Since there were so many people to buy for, they had set a limit of $5 per gift, which meant the gifts were mostly gags. Rachel's gifts included a woven leather bracelet from Eve with Rachel's name on it, earrings that looked like fishhooks from Tyler who explained they were because she liked to hook people up, a huge box of Nerds candy with an unofficial science club membership badge from Tara, a CD Reggie had made that included all his favorite rap songs so she could broaden her musical horizons, an *Insiders Guide to Dr. Who* from Garrett who promised she would love it if she just gave it a chance and offered to come over and watch it with her sometime, and a helmet from Paige who insisted Rachel wear it every time she got in the car from now on to prevent further injury because she couldn't afford to lose any more brain cells. The last gift was a hot pink tee shirt with a unicorn on it from Cameron. When the design was revealed, Rachel and

Paige both stared at it, wide-eyed with shock, glancing back and forth between each other and Cameron.

"It's just like the one you loved so much when you were a kid," Cameron explained, "only in a grown-up size."

"This is exactly like the shirt I had as a kid. I wore it practically every day until I couldn't squeeze into it anymore. It was my favorite shirt," Rachel said in awe. "Where did you find this, Cameron? And how on earth did you know about it?"

Cameron looked confused. "You must have told me about it. I just saw it at the mall and I recognized it."

"How could you have recognized it when you never saw it before? And why would I tell you about that? I haven't even thought about that shirt in ages," Rachel demanded, a bit too harshly.

"I... I don't know." Cameron held up his hands apologetically. "I'm sorry. It just reminded me of you. I can take it back if you don't want it." He hung his head as if he had committed some great atrocity.

"No, you don't need to apologize!" Rachel exclaimed, upset with herself for freaking out and distressing Cameron. "It's awesome, Cameron. Really. I love it!" Impulsively, she jumped up and embraced him, toppling over Garrett's soda in the process and spilling Mountain Dew all over the floor.

She was out of his arms instantly, yelping and flailing about, looking for something to absorb the soda before it soaked into the carpet. The other guests hopped up too and raced to remove valuables from the soda's path as Rachel began sopping up the mess with napkins. It was a one-man job, but feeling the need to help somehow, the teens began cleaning up the rest of the party mess as well, picking up empty plates and cups and throwing away wads of crumpled wrapping paper till the only thing left was the decorations. With the party's momentum disrupted, the guests stood around awkwardly, not sure what to do next, until Garrett's mother texted him that she was on her way to get him. This prompted everyone to say their goodbyes, hugging and wishing each other happy birthday then shrugging into their coats and gathering their gifts. Soon only Paige and Cameron were left.

Paige started taking down streamers in the living room, so Cameron snatched a few more bites from the buffet before carrying the trays to the kitchen. Rachel took the trays from him and began to transfer the leftover food to plastic containers. "You don't have to help clean up, Cameron. You're a guest!".

"I don't mind helping. Besides, as much as I've been here this week, I don't feel like a guest," Cameron replied with a grin. Rachel smiled back happily. Cameron was such a sweetheart.

"I really love the tee shirt, Cameron. Sorry I freaked out on you. It was just such a weird coincidence, you know?"

"Was it a coincidence, Rachel?" Cameron asked seriously, touching her arm to still her as he gazed into her eyes. "Why do I feel like I've known you forever, Rachel? Did we know each other... before?"

"As far as I know, the first words we ever spoke to each other were six days ago in front of Jason's memorial," Rachel replied. "I feel that way too sometimes, but I think it's just because you remind me a lot of somebody I used to be close to."

"That guy Rider? Is that who I remind you of? What happened with him, Rachel? You never really told me," Cameron probed, his brilliant eyes boring into hers.

Rachel flipped her hair behind her shoulder and looked away, breaking the spell. "Because it doesn't matter, Cameron. He's gone."

"Of course it matters, Rachel. He obviously meant a lot to you. You must miss him. I just wonder if you only like me because I remind you of him." Cameron's eyes dropped at the last statement, and he busied himself scraping leftovers into Tupperware.

"That's not true, Cameron! I like you for you. You're kind, and funny, and thoughtful... and gorgeous." Rachel winked, lifting Cameron's face with her finger so she could look into his eyes. "Rider was an amazing person, and you remind me of him because you're amazing, too."

Rachel's body had gotten closer and closer to Cameron's as she spoke till she could feel his breath on her face. He stared longingly into her eyes for a moment, the wheels in his head turning as he decided their fate. It felt completely natural for him to lean in and kiss her. Feeling a spark of electricity so strong it overtook her senses, Rachel's arms wrapped around his waist as she closed the gap between them and kissed him back.

She didn't realize at first that Cameron was struggling to pull away till his lips broke free from hers and he pushed her away violently. A stunned look on his face, Cameron stared at her in confusion and fear. He shook his head as if to deny everything that had just happened then dashed frantically out of the house and into his car. He peeled out of her driveway and into the street without so much as a glance, fortunate that the suburban street was empty at that time of the night.

Chapter Twenty

Cameron tossed and turned in his bed that night, playing the scenes over and over in his mind. Kissing Rachel had opened a floodgate of memories, and he saw his past played out before him like a movie on fast forward, single moments and entire days, glimpses of the life he had lived. Except it wasn't his life, it was Rachel's.

He saw her as a toddler playing happily by herself in her bedroom, meeting Paige as a kindergartener while wearing her unicorn tee, dancing and singing the munchkin song in an elementary school production of The Wizard of Oz, crying as the kids at school teased her, fretting over her first pimple as a teenager, and screaming in terror as her body flew through the window of the crumpled car. In every memory she was talking to him, telling him her feelings, sharing her life, and he was there with her, experiencing it all through her — rejoicing in her happiness and empathizing in her pain. She called him Rider and she was his whole life.

Cameron's mother could hear him, fretting restlessly in his room for hours, and she went to check on him. "Sweetheart," she said quietly, peeking into his room, "is something wrong?"

Cameron sat up and looked at the woman he called mother. He still had no memories of her whatsoever. "Can you tell me some more about my childhood? I still can't remember anything," he asked desperately, trying to ignore the revelation about Rider and make sense of the life he was supposed to have lived.

"Sure, honey." Mrs. Wilson sat down on the bed next to Cameron and brushed her fingers through his hair like she had when he was a child. She told him about his first birthday and how he had squished cake all over his face then threw big handfuls of it at everyone within reach, how anxious he was for his brother and sister to be born so he would have someone to play with, how he loved to play baseball and joined the little league team as soon as he could, how he brought home his first girlfriend at the age of 13 but dumped her soon after because she didn't like video games. The stories amused him and released some of his tension, but they weren't familiar to him at all.

"Mom, did I ever meet Rachel Masterson as a kid?" Cameron asked, interrupting his mother's nostalgia when he realized her stories weren't helping.

"Not that I know of, sweetheart. Didn't you say she just moved here?"

"Yeah, she did," Cameron answered but didn't try

to explain. "I think I'm gonna try to go to sleep now, okay Mom?"

"Okay, honey." Janice smiled and kissed him on the head. When she left, Cameron lay quietly on his bed, pondering, till the sun came up and he decided it was late enough to get up. He puttered around, taking a shower and tidying his room till he couldn't stand it anymore and he gave in and sent Rachel a text.

"I'm sorry about last night. Can we talk?" He typed, hoping he wasn't waking her up.

A few moments later she sent a terse reply, "Yes."

Cameron scribbled a note to his parents and dashed out to his car. Driving way too fast for someone with his track record, just a few minutes later he was at Rachel's door. He rang the bell and waited impatiently for her to open it. His heart was racing and his limbs shook as he paced back and forth on the porch.

"I thought you were going to call," Rachel replied, letting Cameron into the foyer. Her hair was messy from sleeping, and she wore pajamas and a look of apprehension.

"I just... needed to see you," Cameron couldn't begin to explain. "I'm sorry I ran out like that last night. It wasn't about you." Of course it was about her, but not in the way she probably thought.

Rachel was still standing there, looking unsure, so Cameron took the lead and guided her into the living room. The rest of the house was quiet, and Cameron assumed that

Soulmate

Paige was still sleeping up in Rachel's room. They sat face to face on the sofa, knees practically touching, but neither knew how to start.

"You must think I'm a total jerk," Cameron began.

"No, but I don't really understand what happened," Rachel offered, graciously. She had been surprised at first, then confused, then upset, but never really mad. She didn't know what was going on in Cameron's head, but she understood what it was like to feel a whole bunch of conflicting things all at the same time.

"I wasn't upset with you, Rachel. You have to know that. I think you're amazing and I never meant to hurt you."

"I guess I knew that, but it still felt pretty awful," Rachel admitted.

"I'm so sorry, Rachel." Cameron apologized, taking her hand and staring deeply into her eyes. "Please forgive me." Rachel nodded slowly, but her eyes still begged for an explanation.

"Rachel, I ran away last night because something… strange happened when I kissed you."

"Great," Rachel rolled her eyes. "That's the kind of response a girl wants to get when she kisses somebody." Her tone was sarcastic but Cameron knew the hurt was real.

"I got my memory back, Rachel," Cameron quietly revealed.

Rachel's eyes widened in surprise then softened in concern. "That's great, isn't it?" She questioned. He didn't seem as happy about it as she would expect.

"Rachel, who's Rider?" Cameron asked bluntly.

Rachel looked confused at the non sequitur. "He was just a friend, Cameron. I told you. He's gone now."

"Where did he go?" Cameron pushed.

"What does it matter, Cameron? What does this have to do with you? You never even met him," Rachel hedged, a little unnerved at Cameron's inquiry.

"Rachel, please tell me the truth. If you care about me at all I need to hear the whole story," Cameron demanded, sickened by the way he was pressing her to divulge her secrets before he was willing to share his own. What a loser he was, he thought, but he couldn't bring himself to tell her his theory until she confirmed what he believed.

"Cameron, Rider is no threat to you," Rachel insisted. "Can we please just leave it at that?" She begged for understanding with the tone of her voice but Cameron would not be dissuaded.

"Did Rider die, Rachel? Or did he just... disappear? When did it happen, Rachel? Was it because of the accident?"

"Why are you asking me all these questions, Cameron?! Why can't you just leave it alone?" Rachel cried, jumping up from the couch and running into the other room, her head in her hands. Cameron approached her from behind and turned her sobbing body towards his. He held her for a moment while she cried before finally mustering the courage to speak.

"I'm sorry, Rachel. I'm such a jerk," Cameron admitted ruefully, rubbing her back as she buried her head in his shoulder. "It's just, it can't possibly be true, but somehow it is, and I wanted you to say it first so you wouldn't think I was crazy."

"Why would I think you were crazy, Cameron?" Rachel asked hesitantly, turning her tear-stained face up to his.

"Cameron Wilson died on the operating table the night of the accident," Cameron explained solemnly. "His heart stopped beating."

"So did mine, Cameron. But they revived us. They brought us both back," Rachel insisted, not sure where this was going.

"They brought you back, but they didn't bring Rider back, did they?" Cameron's voice was coarse and husky with fear. Rachel stared at him in shock, her face a mask of stoicism as she tried to process what he just said.

"They didn't bring Cameron back, either, Rachel. They revived his body, but his soul was already gone."

"If you're not Cameron then who are you?" Rachel asked, her voice barely a whisper.

"I think you know, Rachel. I think you've sensed it all along. How many times have I reminded you of him?

You hardly even miss him when you're around me, right? It's because he's not gone, Rachel. I've been here all along. I just didn't know who I was." Cameron held Rachel tight as her body began to quiver and her eyes welled up again with tears. Fat drops rolled down her cheeks, but she didn't blink as she stared into his eyes.

"You remembered my favorite shirt," Rachel replied, deliberating. Her emotions threatened to over-whelm her, but she forced herself to think.

"And your favorite party food. And the story about how you used to play house with your cat, Maxie. Just like I knew you liked to watch *The Batchelor* on Monday nights and you prefer daisies over roses. It was all there inside, I just couldn't put it together. I'm not Cameron, Rachel, I'm Rider. I don't remember Cameron's life because I didn't live it. I remember your life. When I kissed you it all came back to me."

Rachel's heart thrummed with excitement at the possibility. Could it really be true? She thought back on all the moments she'd had with Cameron since the accident — the feelings of comfort and familiarity in his presence, the desire to tell him all her secrets and the unexplainable certainty that he would understand, the way he talked smack just like Rider and loved the same silly things like her mother's Dorito casserole and the first and third Shrek movies but not the second or the fourth.

She had never been able to explain how Rider had ended up in her body in the first place, only knew that it was true, so how could she deny the possibility that Rider's soul had made the leap to Cameron when her body had momentarily died? Her mind searched for reasons to discount him, but found only evidence of the truth. With shaking arms she reached up to cradle his face in her hands. She stared intently into his eyes, trying to decipher the mysteries of the universe in their brilliant blue depths. She realized she might never understand how all this had happened, and the only thing she knew for sure was how she felt. She was in love with the boy in front of her ,and in the end that was all the proof she'd ever need.

"Kiss me again, then, and I'll know it's true," Rachel whispered confidently, and Rider swept her up in his arms and kissed her like she'd never been kissed before.

To Be Continued……

Keep reading for a sneak peak of

book 2 in The Soulmate Series!

Follow Rider's journey to understand his past and unlock the secret of his special powers.

<u>A Note from the Author</u>

Dear Reader,
If you enjoyed this book, will you please take one more minute to write a review? Reviews are critical to an author's success, plus they give us the warm fuzzies! It doesn't have to be long or glowing; just a few honest words and a star rating would be awesome!

Now tell your friends!

Now Available!

Soulsearch

The Soulmate Series: Book Two

Who says you can only have one soulmate?

Paige is thrilled when her best friend, Rachel, finds her soulmate in a fairytale love story, but when does she get to be the princess?

When Rachel and her boyfriend go searching for answers to his supernatural beginnings, Paige is happy to help, especially if the quest involves hunky Zach Pasquetti. He seems like her knight in shining armor, but is Zach the villain or is he the prince?

Turn the page for a sneak peek!

Kellie McAllen

Soulsearch

The Soulmate Series

Soulsearch

The Soulmate Series, Book 2

Rachel and Rider lay on Rachel's bed, their arms, legs and lips intwined and their school books scattered on the floor below them where they had fallen minutes after the pair had stacked them on the bed with the intention of studying. Like they usually did after school, the two had gone to Rachel's house to do their homework and spend the evening hanging out, watching their favorite TV shows and telling each other every little detail about their day. Since they now lived separate lives, not knowing what the other was doing every moment was practically unbearable.

Rachel and Rider were soulmates. Not just two people who fell in love and knew they were meant to be together — their souls had cohabited in Rachel's body for 16 years, from before birth until a near-death experience ripped Rider's soul from Rachel's body. Miraculously, Rachel's broken body was revived, and Rider's soul took residence in another form, as Cameron Wilson, a teenage boy whose lifeless body had become an empty shell, kept alive only by machines, since his soul had already passed on.

The incredible tragedy had become their greatest gift, however, allowing Rachel and Rider's relationship to blossom from inseparable friendship into all-consuming love. Although it was maddening for them to be apart from each other, the opportunity to love each other this new way was worth all the pain of their separation. Their passion for each other felt as new and fresh as the thrill of first love, but as strong and committed as lifelong partners. The chance to touch each other, hold each other, and kiss like lovers was an overwhelming pleasure they had never imagined they could experience, and the newness did not seem to be wearing off. Every minute apart was pure torture, but every moment together was ecstasy. It was easy to see why their brief moments of privacy were always spent in each other's arms.

Those precious few hours between school and Rachel's parents' return from work were a tiny window of opportunity to be alone together and had become a little taste of heaven. The school work could wait till the bustle of family time invaded their fantasy world. For now, Rachel marveled in the feel of Rider's hands on her skin, his soft lips on her mouth, his warm breath on her cheek. She ached to join her body completely with his, to be held so close their bodies fused, their skin melting into one flesh. So strange, to feel that way about the person who had until recently been just that, one with her body. But this was better, she thought, holding him impossibly closer. The intense desire to absorb him into herself and the intoxicating feel of his flesh pressed tightly against hers. Rachel could hardly breath for wanting him so badly.

Their intimacy was interrupted by the sound of Rachel's cell phone, blaring out the "Best Friend" by Harry Nilsson ringtone that indicated a call from Paige Donovan, Rachel's BFF since kindergarten and the only person in the world who knew and believed the real story of Rider/Cameron. "Let me guess, you two losers are snogging in your bedroom right about now, aren't you?" Paige said, in lieu of hello.

"Snogging?" Rachel replied, untangling herself from

Rider and putting the phone on speaker so she could straighten her clothes and hair. Rider took the opportunity to tidy their school books and the bed covers so it would not be immediately obvious when Rachel's mom arrived that they had indeed been "snogging" instead of studying.

"It's British slang for kissing, duh!" Paige explained with mock condescension.

"And you know this because.....you've been reading way too many online gossip articles about the One Direction boys?" Rachel retorted.

"Ha ha. Very funny. You're the one with the hots for Louis Tomlinson, aren't you?"

Rachel did have a bit of a crush on the oldest One Direction band member, but only because his shaggy brown hair and blue eyes reminded her of Rider. A little thrill coursed through her when she realized she didn't know what Cameron's singing voice sounded like. Having spent every moment of the first 16 years of their life together, Rachel knew everything about Rider, but Cameron was a stranger to her. It was hard at first to accept that this body now belonged to Rider. Rider's voice had sounded different in her head and the face she pictured when she thought of him was nothing like the face he now wore. This one was better, actually. Cameron had a boyish handsomeness that made Rachel weak at the knees, but unlike most of the other good-looking boys she had met, Rider was too humble to recognize his own attractiveness. He had an adorable habit of dropping his head when he talked to her and peeking out from under the hair that fell over his eyes. He also had a tendency to gaze longingly at her, caressing every inch of her body with his eyes in a way that made her feel like the most desirable girl on the face of the earth.

"Only cuz he looks like my super hot boyfriend, who I

was passionately KISSING when you so rudely interrupted," Rachel teased. "Snogging sounds disgusting, by the way."

"I don't care what you call it, I'd just like to do it," Paige admitted pathetically, pulling on a strand of her curly black hair. Life had not been easy for Paige as Rachel's best friend. Rachel had tried to convince her classmates of the existence of Rider years before and Paige had stood up for her. Consequently, they both had earned a reputation as weird and crazy and had been ostracized from their peers ever since. When Rachel moved 250 miles from Allendale, Michigan, to Indianapolis, Indiana, several months ago, Paige had been left all alone.

"I didn't call to complain about my love life, though, I called to invite you two to my birthday party!" Paige quickly reverted to her normal happy-go-lucky self.

"Name the time and the place, and we'll be there," Rachel promised, feeling confident to speak for Rider too. Rachel had revealed the truth about Rider to Paige when they were only five years old, and with childlike faith Paige had accepted him, sight unseen. Rider appreciated Paige because she talked to him — not just to Rachel, but directly to him, including him in the relationship like there was no doubt he was real. It never seemed to bother her that she couldn't see his face or hear his voice. Rachel spoke his thoughts aloud to Paige when they were together, and Paige had come to know Rider's personality as well as she knew Rachel's. Paige and Rider had a similar tendency towards sass and sarcasm, and they played off each other hilariously.

"Next weekend," Paige replied excitedly. "Come down Friday after school if you want and stay the whole weekend. My parents are cool with it. Do you think

Cameron's will be, Rider?"

Rider wasn't sure about that. Taking over someone else's body had come with a unique set of complications. Outwardly, he was Cameron Wilson, and he lived with Cameron's family and pretended to be the son they knew and loved. Cameron's memory vanished when his soul departed, though, and Rider knew very little about the person he was pretending to be. His parents believed he had amnesia as a result of his accident, so they tried to be understanding, but he knew they mourned the loss of their son, even though they didn't realize he was truly gone. Rider was constantly surprising them with his un-Cameron-like behavior, and their family dynamic was so different from Rachel's that Rider never quite knew what to expect from them.

"I will use my charm and wit to persuade them," Rider promised hopefully. He really was eager to see Paige again.

The three chatted for a few more minutes before Rachel sensed that something was on Rider's mind. "Okay, spill it, Rider. I can tell you're stewing about something."

Rider looked earnestly at Rachel hoping she would understand as he began describing the idea he had been contemplating for several weeks. "I've been thinking a lot about what happened to me, and I've been trying to figure out why it happened," Rider began, his excitement growing with each sentence. "I didn't have a clue before, why we were the way we were. I guess I just assumed we were supposed to be twins or something and I just never grew my own body. But after the accident, I wondered." Rider's face lit up as he explained his current theory. "I think I left your body when your heart stopped on the operating table, and I believe I entered Cameron's body because his soul was already gone, but his body was still alive. It was all about the timing. And proximity. He was in the same place at the same time. So I started wondering, maybe I was in a different body first, maybe my own body, but it died, and somehow I jumped into yours before you were born!"

"So, you think maybe you lived another whole life before you joined me?" Rachel asked, her voice a mix of surprise and concern. She didn't know why the thought of that bothered her.

"No. I mean, I don't know. I don't think so. I don't have any memories of a life before you, but maybe I just lost them, like I lost my memory when I entered Cameron."

"But you got those memories back eventually."

"Yeah, and they all came back, clear as ever. So I'm wondering if…"

"You were just a baby!" Paige interrupted excitedly, fascinated by the theory.

"That's what I was thinking, too," Rider agreed. "Maybe I was an infant, or even a fetus, and I was miscarried, or aborted. That would explain why I don't remember a past life."

"I can see how you could take over Cameron's body, since he was gone, but how could you enter mine when I was alive?" Rachel wondered, intrigued but not convinced.

"I'm not sure, maybe I didn't. Or maybe you were just an easy vessel to enter because you were so young, or weak or something," Rider offered, no easy explanation at hand.

"Those are all really interesting ideas, Rider, but I don't see how you could possibly find out the truth."

"Well, Paige just gave me an idea," Rider replied excitedly.

"I did?" Paige asked incredulously.

"Well, not exactly, but you gave me an opportunity anyway. I was thinking maybe we could do some snooping..." Rider went on to describe a convoluted plan that involved sneaking into the women's clinic where Rachel's mother had received prenatal care, in hopes of perusing their records system to determine if any other women had lost babies at the same time as Rachel's mother had been receiving care.

"But how do you know it happened at the clinic?" Rachel asked, confused and dismayed by this strange new Rider. She hadn't realized how much thought he had given to his peculiar situation. She knew it was unique, this symbiosis they shared, but she had always just accepted it as part of who she was, who they were. She was surprised to realize Rider didn't feel the same way. It felt almost like betrayal, like the life they had lived wasn't enough for him anymore.

"I don't know. I don't really know anything. It's just a wild guess at this point. But it's a place to start anyway. And Paige's birthday gives us a perfect excuse to go back there, to Allendale."

Rachel could tell that Paige was thrilled at this new development. She always had been more spontaneous than Rachel, more of a risk-taker, always looking for some kind of excitement to spice up her life. Rachel was happy with the status quo and preferred the safe over the unknown, but she could see the excitement shining in Rider's eyes as he described his plan and she knew she could never deny him. They finished the conversation on a high, jabbering happily about the upcoming party and making promises to contemplate strategies for the mission ahead.

When the phone call was over, Rider took Rachel in

his arms, his face alight with anticipation. As he kissed her, Rachel's mind was awhirl, but she felt the passion building up inside her, and she longed for a way to release it. She wanted more than just kisses and Rider's tender embrace.

"Rider," she spoke seriously, pulling away from his kiss to look him in the eye. "I have an idea for how to get into the women's clinic. Besides sneaking, I mean." Rider raised an eyebrow in speculation. "What if I just make an appointment and you go with me?" Rachel offered.

"Rachel, that's a great idea! Why didn't I think of that?! I guess I was just caught up in the possibility of espionage! But that makes so much more sense. I still might have to sneak in some other time to access their records, but going there for an appointment would give me a chance to do some reconnaissance first. So what kind of appointment could you set up? I guess you could just say you're having some lady problems." Rider's face bunched up in revulsion as he considered the scope of possible problems a female could have.

"I actually had something else in mind," Rachel's eyes gazed hopefully into Rider's.

"Like what?" Rider asked, confused by the hesitation in her voice and the apprehensive look on her face.

"Like birth control," Rachel admitted bashfully, dropping her eyes into her lap, their jean-clad knees touching as they sat facing each other on the bed.

Rider took her hands in his and squeezed, his heart thumping wildly in his chest. "Rachel? What are you saying?" he asked, a lump in his throat.

"I'm saying I love you, Rider, and I want to show you any way I can." Rachel's eyes shimmered with unshed tears, evidence of the intense emotions churning inside her.

Rider's first response was to grab her and make love to her with all the passion of a thousand lifetimes, but instead he simply took her cheek in his hand and placed a gentle kiss on her lips. "I love you too, Rachel. More than you can possibly imagine. I love you so much it hurts just to think about it. And there's nothing I'd like more than to be with you that way, but...are you sure that's what you want?" His voice had dropped to a whisper as he stared deeply into her eyes, trying to see through to her soul.

"I'm sure about you, Rider. I've never been more sure about anything in my whole life. I want to be with you forever. I don't ever want to lose you, Rider. I want to have all of you."

"You never have to worry about losing me, Rachel. I'm yours for eternity. I always have been," Rider declared and brought his lips down to hers....

Now available!

About the Author

Kellie McAllen is a bibliophile who has her nose in a book every moment she can. When she's not reading or writing she's either baking cupcakes, obsessively decorating and redecorating her home, or watching reality dance shows on TV. She lives in North Carolina with her husband, her teenage daughter, and 2 cats.

Keep up with Kellie at:
www.kelliemcallen.com

CPSIA information can be obtained
at www.ICGtesting.com
Printed in the USA
FSOW02n0723051216
28177FS